AVALON
QUEST FOR MAGIC

BOOK 3

Ghost Wolf

Other books in the Avalon series by Rachel Roberts

AVALON

QUEST FOR MAGIC

BOOK 3

Ghost Wolf

by Rachel Roberts

red sky
publishing

C·S Books
New York

"Earth Song" Written by Debra Davis © 2004
Big Old Soul Music (ASCAP).
Lyrics used by permission.

For more information, address
CDS Books
425 Madison Avenue
New York, NY 10017
(212) 223-2969, Fax (212) 223-1504

First Edition.

ISBN: 1-59315-012-1

Cover Illustration by Jim Carroll
Cover Design by Richard Aquan

10 9 8 7 6 5 4 3 2 1

THE WORLD OF AVALON

The Mages:

Emily The healer, wears the rainbow jewel

Adriane The warrior, wears the wolf stone

Kara The blazing star, wears the unicorn jewel

Ozzie An elf trapped in the body of a ferret, wears the ferret stone

Three teenagers and a ferret whose lives crisscross at the intersection of magic and friendship. Together they fight the dark powers bent on controlling the home of all magic, a mystical place called Avalon.

Magical Animal Friends:

Lyra Winged leopard cat bonded to Kara

Dreamer Mistwolf bonded to Adriane

Stormbringer Mistwolf bonded to Adriane

Ariel Magical owl

Starfire Elemental fire stallion bonded to Kara

Dragonflies Mini dragons, Goldie, Blaze, Barney, Fiona, and Fred

The Drake Dragon bonded to Zach and Adriane

❀ ❀ ❀ ❀ ❀ ❀ ❀ ❀ ❀ ❀

Aldenmor:

Fairimentals	Protectors of the magic of Aldenmor, take form in different elements
Tweek	Experimental earth Fairimental sent to mentor the mages
Zach	A teenage boy raised by mistwolves, wears the dragon stone

Home Base:
The Ravenswood Animal Preserve

The Dark Mages:

The Spider Witch	Elemental magic master
The Dark Sorceress	Half human, half animal magic user

The Quest:
Return nine missing power crystals to Avalon. Without these crystals, the magical secrets of Avalon will be lost forever.

❀ ❀ ❀ ❀ ❀ ❀ ❀ ❀ ❀ ❀

Chapter 1

The full moon rose, illuminating the forests of Ravenswood with a cold silver glow. Adriane Charday stood surrounded by the mass of great trees. She could not stop the memories, vivid with pain and terror, from flashing through her mind. The dreams of her first pack mate were always the same: Stormbringer sacrificing herself to save the other mistwolves, and Adriane powerless to help her.

The musky scent of fear filled her senses, a palpable trail on the soft breeze. She swung around, knowing that a doe and her yearling fawn were hiding in the brush behind her.

Somewhere in the distance a wolf howled—a high, keening note that quickly descended in pitch. Instinctively, Adriane raised her face to the moon and howled. Another joined in, and then a chorus echoing through the trees. Mistwolves!

But something was wrong.

The pack was lost, separated from its home. Adriane stood for a moment, listening. She knew what it was like to be lost and alone.

The golden wolf stone burned upon her wrist.

A mournful, sliding yowl thrummed through her. Adriane recognized the call instantly. The mistwolves were in danger. She had to help!

Her black eyes gleamed as she charged through the undergrowth, wildly dodging low-hanging oak branches and leaping over fallen logs. She felt her lips draw back in a snarl.

Suddenly, the forests around her started rippling and distorting. Earthy browns and greens shifted into bizarre blues and reds. Majestic trees took on jagged shapes as their colors wavered into ghostly purple hues. Even the familiar forest scents of pine and loam were lost in this unnatural wood.

Panic ripped through her. What was happening?

Adriane plunged ahead, ignoring the sharp brambles, as the forests lurched around her, warping into brilliant pinks and ambers. Terrified, she cried out for help, but only a ragged howl tore from her throat.

The familiar scent of her first pack mate filled her sharply enhanced senses, making her heart pound.

Then her wolf senses were picking up something else, as if the forest itself were calling to her, calming her magic.

Something flashed in the distance. Her vision, sharpened with wolf's eyes, locked onto a tower of bright light glowing in the depths of the trees. She ran toward it.

Adriane barreled headlong into an open glade,

drawn by feelings that she could not name. She looked up at the massive stone tower, its pinnacle pointing like a thin finger to the sky.

The Rocking Stone. She was in the magic glade of Ravenswood. Willow trees bordering the lake glowed within the stone's light, their golden bark pulsing with power.

A song, rising and falling like a mother's lullaby, drifted across the glade. Adriane closed her eyes, feeling the magic with her wolf senses, letting the melody soothe her.

"I have been waiting for you, warrior."

Adriane swung around, jewel light slashing across her eyes like fire. "Who's there?"

A willow tree near the lakeshore moved, rippling the radiant waters of the lake.

Adriane approached cautiously and saw her—what appeared to be a tree was a figure, a fairy creature. Adriane knew instinctively that this was the source of the glade's magic, the heart of Ravenswood. The extraordinary figure raised her head, grassy hair flowing down her back in long curling strands of green and brown. Sinuous branches unfurled into long arms stretching wide to embrace the glade and the surrounding forests. Moonlight danced across bright flowers dotting her gown of velvety moss. Slender legs twisted down into strong roots.

The forest creature turned her head expectantly, luminous eyes shifting from greens to blues to browns, reflecting all the colors of the forest. Spotting Adriane, a smile as bright as sunlight spread across her beautiful features. *"I have watched you with great joy, young warrior."*

The voice flowed through Adriane, filling her with the sweetness of life.

"Who—what are you?"

"I am Orenda, a sylph bonded to these forests," the figure said stiffly, as if the effort to speak were painful.

Bonded to the forests? Adriane and her friends, Emily and Kara, certainly knew about bonding with magical animals. It was essential to using their magical abilities. But this was something entirely different.

Adriane looked closer. Silken threads snaked through the willow's branches, forming a net that cut like wire. Green oozed from split bark, dripping like blood.

The sylph's face twisted in agony as the webbing tightened.

Adriane gasped, her heart twisted by the sylph's pain. "What's happening to you?"

"I am sick."

A profound sadness swept through Adriane.

"I cannot protect my forest," the wondrous creature said, her voice like a soft breeze. *"It is now up to you."*

Suddenly, webbing surged from the shadows, ensnaring Orenda's willowy arms. The sylph jerked forward, grassy hair crackling. An immense cocoon was forming around her.

Adriane swooned as dizzying waves of dark magic attacked the forest sylph. Gleaming strands closed tight, crushing the sylph's graceful limbs with sickening cracks.

Adriane desperately summoned her magic, her wolf stone casting a blaze of light across the glade. "Tell me what to do!"

Orenda's voice was urgent. *"The ones that are lost must be found."*

"Who is lost?"

"The mistwolves," the sylph whispered, the song of life all but crushed from her breath.

Mistwolves? The mistwolves were on Aldenmor. "I don't understand."

A vicious snarl rumbled from the woods.

Adriane swung into a fighting stance as wolf eyes materialized in the gloom, glittering malevolently.

"Storm?" she called out in a panic.

The ghostly figure crept from the trees, circling the warrior. The mistwolf was massive. It didn't look real. Cold blue light shimmered through its translucent body. One eye glowed blue, the other green. Silver teeth bared, lips pulled back, the creature snarled the death grin of a hunting wolf.

"You do not belong with the wolves," it challenged. *"A wolf protects the pack."*

"Who are you?" Adriane tensed, torn between fleeing and fighting.

"I am the pack leader," the wolf snarled.

"This is *my* home," Adriane said, her wolf stone blazing in warning. "You are the intruder."

The wolf circled, smelling its victim's fear.

"I don't want to hurt you." Adriane raised her jewel, sparks of light edging along her arm.

"It is your nature, human. You will always hurt the mistwolves."

Jaws snapping, the pack leader rushed in without warning, his shoulder ramming Adriane's left side. Savage magic hit her like an electric shock. The wolf stone exploded in golden light.

"No!" The air rushed from Adriane's chest as the massive wolf pinned her to the ground. She tried to move, but her legs and arms were held motionless. Struggling, she rolled over and fell, landing hard.

Suddenly her eyes flew open, though she hadn't realized they were closed. Something black as night loomed over her, a snarling shadow barely visible in the darkness. Screaming, she rolled away, desperately trying to free her wolf stone and defend herself.

The wolf's wild emerald eyes locked onto her panicked gaze as she wrenched her wrist free, wolf stone sparking dangerously.

"Dreamer?" Adriane breathed.

Her pack mate's jet-black fur gleamed, the snowy star upon his chest reflecting the gold of her magic.

The mistwolf nosed twisted blankets away from her arms and legs, snapping at the air, his hackles raised.

"Dreamer!" Adriane's hands flew to protect her face. "It's okay. It's me," she reassured her pack mate, taking in the familiar scene of her own room. It had only been a dream.

The dreamcatchers over her bed caught the moonlight, casting shadows like spiderwebs.

"Pack mate." Dreamer's voice sounded faintly in her mind, as if he were having trouble communicating.

"Easy." Adriane knelt and grabbed the wolf gently by the ears and stared at him, nose to nose. "Shhh. It's okay."

She held her friend close, feeling his heart pounding against her own.

She felt the wolf trying to speak, his thoughts brushing at the edge of her mind.

"What's wrong?" Adriane asked, concentrating on the jagged connection.

Dreamer stood back, his tail between his legs, ears flattened. No longer snarling, he tilted his head to one side, embarrassed and uncertain.

A cold fear rushed through her. Something was wrong with his magic.

Snarling in frustration, the wolf sent a flurry of jumbled images crashing into her mind.

The forests of Ravenswood twisting and warping—

dark creatures hunting in the pale starlight—her grand-mother, motionless, slumped over the kitchen table—the sickly gleam of a terrifying spiderweb—

"Dreamer!" Adriane gasped, reeling from the impact of the horrible images. "Is there something wrong with Gran?"

Dreamer raised his nose and barked, confirming her fear. Adriane leaped to her feet and raced out of her bedroom, Dreamer on her heels. Fear was thick in her throat as she sped down the stairs and skidded into the kitchen.

"Gran!" she cried.

Just as in Dreamer's vision, her grandmother sat at the round wooden table, slumped over a cup of tea.

The old woman looked up slowly as Adriane rushed to her side, her face pale and drawn. "Little Bird . . ."

"Gran, are you all right?" Adriane asked.

Gran smiled weakly and gestured to the chair opposite hers. Silver and turquoise bracelets clanked on her thin wrists. Adriane turned and saw hot cocoa steaming in her favorite blue mug, as if Gran had expected her.

Dreamer lay down near the table, head resting on his paws.

Sitting down, Adriane closed her hands tightly around the warm drink and studied her grandmother. Nakoda Charday had always been so vital and full of life, it was impossible to mark her with age. But now, deep lines ran from her eyes, creasing her weathered, dark skin like patches of worn leather. Her black eyes were sunken and glassy. Adriane breathed deeper. She had never seen Gran look so—old.

Gran drew her long white braid over her shoulder. Her tired eyes sharpened and focused on Adriane. "The forest spirit is dying."

"The forest spirit?" Adriane echoed. First Dreamer had shown her images from her nightmare, and now it seemed Gran knew about the sylph.

Gran nodded. "I know you feel it, too, Little Bird. The forest called to you."

Adriane fought to appear calm, but her heart was racing. It had been over a year since her parents had first brought her to Ravenswood, but the memory was still fresh. The forest had called to her then as well. It had given her something wonderful. She watched her grandmother study the gem upon Adriane's wrist. The golden wolf stone pulsed with light.

"Do you know why I insisted your mother bring you here?" Gran asked.

Adriane shrugged, her long black hair falling over her face. "She and Dad were busy touring with their art."

Gran shook her head. "Your mother never had the gift. But you do."

"The forest spirit was just a dream," Adriane insisted. "Wasn't it?"

"Just because it was a dream doesn't mean it's not real," Gran said, a shadow of a smile deepening the wrinkles around her eyes and mouth. Her long, slender fingers reached out and covered Adriane's precious stone of magic. "I was right to bring you here."

Startled, Adriane regarded the jewel on her black and turquoise wristband. She had found the wolf stone in the forests of Ravenswood not long after she had come to live here. Was it all supposed to happen this way? Had she been destined to meet Storm? And then to lose her?

Gritting her teeth against the tears that always threatened when she thought about Storm, she looked down at her hands. And froze. Black dirt streaked her fingers and nails. Her blue T-shirt and sweatpants were covered with grass stains and mud.

Frantically, she pushed up the right leg of her pants. Streaks of dried blood marked her ankle— where she had run through the brambles in her dream. Or what she thought had been a dream.

"The wolves . . . they call to me, Gran," she told her grandmother quietly, head bowed. "Sometimes . . . I dream about running with them and never coming back."

Gran nodded, her grip tightening on Adriane's wrist.

"It seems Little Bird has found her true name," Gran said. "Little Wolf."

Chapter 2

The golden brown ferret's voice echoed though the Ravenswood Manor library as Adriane walked in.

"Listen, my friends, to this wondrous tale," Ozzie read dramatically, arms waving, nose twitching:

> *"Of a hero whose courage would not fail.*
> *"When all seemed lost and our fate tragic,*
> *"Along came a princess of strong heart and magic.*
> *"With her jewel of power and fiery steed,*
> *"She saved the Fairy Realms in its hour of need.*
> *"She came from afar, she didn't come in a car,*
> *"This was the ride of the blazing star!"*

"Hooo." Ariel, a magical snow owl, nodded her feathery head, blinking her giant sky blue eyes. She was perched on the library ladder admiring Kara's dazzling unicorn jewel. Sun streamed through the huge bay windows, sending sparkles of white, pink, and red dancing across the high-domed ceiling of the grand library.

"*Not bad,*" Lyra, a leopard-like cat, said, washing her shoulder with long licks.

"What is that, Ozzie?" Emily asked, walking over to the computer console. The workstation was set behind a secret panel in the library wall. Ozzie had officially become the computer expert mage, ordering supplies for the preserve online, as well as handling all the e-mail.

"E-mail from the Fairy Realms," Ozzie reported, his golden ferret stone shining on his leather collar. "Lyrics for 'The Ballad of the Blazing Star.' "

"Looks like you made quite an impression, as usual." The red-haired healer smiled at Kara, then turned to Adriane. "Hey, Adriane. What do you think of the blazing ballad?"

With a grunt, Adriane plopped on the couch, propping her boots on the long oak table.

"Are you okay?" Emily asked.

"Just a little tired."

Gran still wasn't feeling any better, and Dreamer had been agitated all morning. Adriane had been up early, checking the glade. In the light of day, everything seemed normal. No sign of the magical tree sylph. But she knew something was wrong. Seeing all her friends busy in the sunlit library made her hesitant to say anything—especially when she wasn't even sure what to think herself.

Adriane brushed her hair away from her face and concentrated on calling Dreamer. The mistwolf, a natural magic tracker, was canvassing the rest of the preserve. He would sniff out anything dangerous.

Holding her wolf stone, she called with her mind, *"Dreamer, where are you?"*

Jagged sparks flashed through Adriane's mind.

"I've never seen anything like it!" Tweek exclaimed, perching next to Ariel. Tweek was a small, magical being composed of earth elements. He had been assigned by the Fairimentals to mentor the mages, an Experimental Fairimental. With Kara's help, Tweek had augmented his leafy stick-figure body with flowers and vines.

"It's incredible, isn't it?" Kara's blue eyes sparkled as she twirled the glittering red, white, and pink gem attached to its silver chain.

"I must say, this is the most impressive jewel I've ever seen," Tweek proclaimed, his twiggy body rattling with excitement. "Of course, I've only been around for six weeks."

"What does it mean, Tweek?" Emily asked.

"It means you are now a Level Two blazing star," Tweek told Kara excitedly, his quartz eyes glistening.

"Yeah, and it totally matches every outfit I own!" The blazing star held the jewel next to her sporty pink running pants, jean jacket, and denim hat embroidered with the Ravenswood logo.

"That's an accomplishment," Lyra observed, green eyes twinkling.

"It usually takes years to advance to Level Two.

You did it in two days." Tweek's quartz eyes rattled. "You're breaking all the rules!"

"Not the first time," Kara quipped.

"You mean our jewels can change more than once?" Emily asked, studying her rainbow healing gem encased on its silver band.

"Yes, every time you move up a rank, your jewel evolves to match your magic," the E. F. explained.

Kara twirled her unicorn jewel. "Mine changed after I bonded with Starfire."

Adriane sat forward, absently rubbing her wolf stone.

The jewel had been rough and unpolished when she first found it in the portal field. But as she and Stormbringer became pack mates, it had quickly transformed into a paw-shaped wolf stone.

"Level One mages use jewels to focus the magic," Tweek explained, looking at Kara. "Bonding with magical animals is essential, protecting you from losing yourself in the magic. But Kara has also bonded with an elemental creature, Starfire. A firemental, no less—inconceivable!"

"And she saved my tail in the nick of time." Lyra rubbed against Kara's side.

"You're welcome," Kara purred.

Adriane felt a pang of sadness watching Kara and Lyra, a Level Two mage and her loving, bonded animal, together forever.

"Level Two mages find their own unique elemental magic based on one of the four elements: water, air, fire, and earth," Tweek continued. "To reach Level Two, a mage must bond with a powerful creature of the same element like Kara did. It's called a paladin."

"What's the difference between a magical animal and a paladin?" Emily asked.

"Magical animals work side by side with you, and are friends that grow with you through all stages of magic," the E. F. answered. "The tie is extremely deep and unbreakable."

Adriane's wolf stone flared. Emily turned concerned hazel eyes to the warrior, sensing her friend's grief.

"A paladin like Kara's fire stallion is a creature made of pure elemental magic," Tweek continued. "Starfire is inextricably linked to Kara and her jewel. Only she can summon him."

"Really?" Kara asked excitedly, waving her sparkling jewel wildly in the air. "Starfire! Heeere, Starfire!"

"No, no." Tweek shook his twigs. "A paladin only comes when you are in great need. It is a protector of immeasurable power."

"Oh." Kara dropped her jewel, frowning.

"Well, Kara," Emily said. "You were the last to find your jewel, but now you're first."

"Exactly where I should be," Kara said, radiating a dazzling smile.

Adriane crossed her arms and sat back, glowering.

Kara, the blazing overachiever. Things always went her way. Adriane had found her jewel first. She had bonded with Storm first. She had worked on her magic for a full year, and now it seemed she was only going backward.

Adriane abruptly stood and started pacing, her shadow casting strange shapes across the inlaid wooden floor. "Could it ever go the opposite way?"

"What do you mean?" Tweek asked.

"Could the jewels ever get *out* of tune?" Adriane held up her wrist, emphasizing her point with a flash from her wolf stone. "Could we lose our magic?"

"Well, technically your magic is always changing. But as you grow more powerful, the greater the chance it could be corrupted. That's why you have your animal friends. To keep you balanced and grounded."

"I lost my bonded animal," Adriane said flatly.

"I lost my magic, and Starfire helped me get it back," Kara said.

"Adriane and I switched magic powers," Emily said.

"We still have some of each other's magic," the warrior added.

Tweek scratched his mossy head. "Frankly, you mages are entering uncharted areas. With the magic flowing wild from Avalon, extraordinary things are happening. That's precisely why the Fairimentals designed me to stay on Earth."

"Incoming." Ozzie turned back to the computer as it *dinged*. "Kara, your e-mail from the city council."

"Perfect. Print it." Kara grabbed her pink Palm-Pilot and started checking her to-do lists. "Tour bus arrives in twenty minutes, people!"

Today was the opening day of the new tourist season. Kara had convinced her dad, the mayor of Stonehill, to add Ravenswood as a stop for a bus touring company. This was a major break for Ravenswood and the girls. As part of their arrangement with the town council, the girls needed to generate income to keep the preserve open.

In the year since the girls had managed the preserve, with the help of Gran and Emily's mom, Dr. Carolyn Fletcher, the animals had flourished. There were more deer than ever, peacocks, all kinds of wild birds, foxes, rabbits, and even a few bears.

That didn't include the special guests who'd decided to stay after the mages healed their home world, Aldenmor. The magical animals helped the mages care for the preserve and monitor for any signs of unusual magical activity.

With a soft hum, a color print slid from the printer.

"Tah-dah!" Kara grabbed the brochure and read it excitedly. " 'Ghosts, witches, monsters! See for yourself if the legends of Ravenswood are real. The Ravenswood Experience—see it, feel it, touch it!' Pretty cool, huh?"

"Hooyaaa!" Ariel cheered.

"We should be focusing on the animals," Adriane said, annoyed.

"It's just a little spin. Besides, it was the only way I could cement the tour deal."

"Maybe it should say, 'You'll be smitten. Not bitten,' " Adriane grumbled.

"Look, the animals are here," Kara pointed out. " 'Lyra the leopard, Dreamer the wolf, and—Ozzie the wonder ferret?' "

Ozzie brushed his cowlick back. "It's all good."

He suddenly jumped, ferret stone flashing, whiskers vibrating. "The tour bus just pulled through the front gates!" he announced.

"Wait." Kara held Lyra's face, moving it left, then right, carefully smoothing the spotted fur. "Perfect." She kissed Lyra's head and stood. "Time to make some magic."

"Into the great unknown," Adriane sighed, following the group out the door.

❧   ❧   ❧

"Ravenswood Manor was built in seventeen fifty-three," Kara said as she led the group of tourists through the immense foyer of the amazing Gothic manor house.

The group consisted of about twenty ladies and a few camera-laden hubbies who had booked the tour as part of a day trip from Atlantic City. Emily and

Adriane were at the rear of the group, ushering the stragglers along.

"Everything in the manor has animal themes," Kara continued, "some more fanciful than others."

The group passed an ornate mahogany table with carvings of unicorns, centaurs, and dragons, which ended in big, clawed feet.

Several women lagged behind, observing every detail.

"Take your time," Kara said, then touched her unicorn jewel, sending a telepathic message to Adriane and Emily. *"Move 'em along!"*

"These paintings are just wonderful," a woman cooed, admiring the many pieces depicting the history of Ravenswood and the animals that had made their home there.

"Ravenswood has always been an animal sanctuary," Emily piped up from the back. "Through the years, different caretakers have kept it in excellent condition, as you can see."

"This is the most recent caretaker, Henry Gardener," Kara said, pointing to a large painting of a handsome man proudly showing off a pair of white tigers.

"Where exactly is Mr. Gardener?" a man asked, snapping photos of the painting.

"He's—" Kara faltered.

"On vacation," Adriane said quickly.

"We heard he mysteriously disappeared," the man persisted.

"Murdered in the cellar with an ax, he was," his wife chimed in.

"Which is the most haunted room?" a woman in all black asked.

"That would be . . . um . . . this room." Kara pointed to the wide living room with the massive marble fireplace and green velvet and mahogany couches.

"This is a unique part of Stonehill's history," a *Stonehill Gazette* reporter said, directing her photographer to snap photos of portraits hung about the formal room. "Legends have it there have always been ghosts and monsters in these woods."

"This place sure looks like it could be haunted," opined a pale, blue-haired woman.

"Who knows what happens when the darkness of night falls and the full moon rises?" the blazing ham said dramatically.

"This is stupid!" Adriane complained to Emily.

Emily shrugged. *"Everyone seems to be enjoying themselves."*

"What about the ghosts?" asked a visitor.

"Okay, I'll tell you a really scary secret," Kara said, warming to her subject as the group crowded around her. "One time, we hosted this big rock star, Johnny Conrad . . ."

"Yes?"

"And I sang a song that died a horrible death."

Adriane snorted.

"What's going on in there?" Ozzie complained to the mages through his ferret stone. *"We're all waiting."*

"You've seen some of our regular guests," Emily said, leading the group through the hallway and toward the rear exit of the manor. "Deer, peacocks, hawks—even parrots. And now it's time to meet our special animals."

Kara flung open the tall double doors to the grand marble patio. Beyond were the water gardens and rose gardens sprawled majestically across the great lawn. Tables on the patio were laden with ice cream, chips, sodas, and cookies.

"Meet Lyra," Kara called out. "A rare leopard breed from, uh . . . France!"

Right on cue, Lyra leaped over a hedge bordering the patio and came to a stop a few feet away from the group. Her sleek orange-spotted fur shimmered in the sun.

"Wow, a real leopard!" someone shouted.

Cameras starting clicking as Kara walked up to Lyra and put out her hand.

Lyra roared, raising a few gasps from the group.

Kara petted the cat, smiling brilliantly.

The group clapped, then gasped as Ozzie sprang from the water gardens and tumbled across the lawns. Lyra leaped to meet Ozzie as he jumped onto her back, juggling pinecones in his furry paws.

"Adorable!" a lady proclaimed, clapping her pink-gloved hands enthusiastically.

Kara laughed. *"Nice touch, guys."*

The acrobatic ferret tossed the cones high in the air one at a time for the dazzling finale.

A piercing howl cut across the lawn, startling everyone. Lyra swung around, sending Ozzie and his cones flying onto the picnic table.

A spike of fear drove through Adriane.

"Is that the wolf?" a lady asked, peering through her horn-rimmed glasses.

"His name is Dreamer, and he's coming right out," Adriane said, looking expectantly to her left, where the pup was supposed to make his entrance from behind a cluster of rosebushes. "I *said*, the wolf is coming right out."

After a long pause, Dreamer slunk from behind a thick violet rosebush. His hackles were on end, and he growled low in his throat.

"Say, he looks meaner than an overfried corn dog," a tourist observed.

Lyra eyed the wolf warily. *"Something is not right with Dreamer."*

With a snarl, Dreamer lunged at the cat. Lyra easily dodged his snapping jaws and stepped back.

Emily and Adriane both ran to the wolf, herding him back from the group.

"Dreamer?" Adriane gasped—her wolf stone was pulsing golden, a warning of danger.

"Easy, Dreamer." Emily's jewel glowed blue as she sent calming magic to the agitated mistwolf. "He's not feeling well," she called back to the tour.

"Are you sure these animals are safe?" one of the ladies demanded.

Adriane tried to respond, but Dreamer jumped between her and the visitors, barking protectively.

The tourists started yelling with alarm.

"Dreamer!" Adriane cried. She wrestled the wolf down, holding his head steady, and looked deep into his green eyes. "What is it? "

Images of gleaming claws, snapping fangs, and spiderwebs barraged her mind as Dreamer thrashed, trying to get away.

"Hooooray!" Ariel zoomed from the skies for her part in the show, cooing happily. Dreamer broke free of Adriane's grasp and lunged at the snow owl.

"Hoo-aahhhh!" Screeching, Ariel careened into the air, narrowly avoiding the mistwolf's teeth and barreling into three tourists.

"Help!" the old lady in horn-rimmed glasses shrieked.

"Yes, help yourselves to cookies and ice cream," Kara shouted as she plucked a pistachio-soaked ferret from a gallon tub. She shot a concerned look to Adriane.

"Dreamer, stop it!" Adriane grabbed the wolf's collar, golden light flashing from her gem.

"This is front-page material," the reporter exclaimed, snapping photos of Dreamer and Adriane.

Adriane looked at Emily desperately. "Take him to Gran—I can't get through to him."

"Dreamer is just a little overexcited about the new season," Emily blurted to the tourists, her jewel shimmering as she pulled him away.

The wolf gave Adriane one last concerned glance before following Emily.

Adriane watched him go, wishing her dark dreams had vanished with the night.

❧　❧　❧

The large chamber shimmered with movement as hundreds of spiders slid along silken strands, weaving subtle colors into the giant tapestry. An intricate landscape of woods and gardens formed beneath their skittering feet.

"This will be my greatest creation." The Spider Witch waved long fingers, her bloodred jewel pulsing upon its ornate spiderwebbed ring. "A masterpiece of dark magic."

A tall figure, startling silver hair draped below her shoulders, stepped from the shadows. "It is an impressive decoration," the Dark Sorceress allowed, her green animal eyes narrowed.

The Spider Witch spun around, moving quickly despite the heavy black robes shrouding her bulky body. "The forest sylph will become a most powerful demon when this weaving is complete."

The Dark Sorceress raised an eyebrow. After so many months in the Otherworlds, her own magic remained weak and drained. Yet the Spider Witch had been trapped there for many years. How could she be so powerful? There had to be a source feeding her magic.

"We must do more if we hope to eliminate the warrior," the Dark Sorceress said.

"You presume to give me advice?" the Spider Witch mocked. "Let me remind you that *your* attempts to harness the magic of the unicorns, the dragons, *and* the mistwolves all failed miserably."

The Dark Sorceress gritted her vampire teeth. If not for that silver mistwolf, she would have harnessed the power of all the mistwolves and the magic of Avalon itself.

"You don't know these girls like I do. You have to go for the heart—the animals," the sorceress shot back. "Everything the warrior loves must be stripped away, her spirit broken."

The Spider Witch directed a mass of black spiders to weave the next image on the tapestry: the cottage house next to the manor. The witch's insect eyes flashed yellow from the depths of her hood as she faced the Dark Sorceress.

"Then let it begin."

"Come again tomorrow!" Kara waved to the tour bus and newspaper van as they sped out of the preserve, leaving the mages and animals standing in a cloud of dust.

"This is a disaster!" she wailed, pushing aside the rainbow-colored balloons bending sadly over the welcome sign.

"All that mint chip!" Ozzie cried.

"Ozzie, let's store the food back in the manor freezer," Emily said.

Suddenly, a fierce howl cut through the air.

"Dreamer?" Adriane called, looking nervously toward the cottage.

Jagged lights pierced her mind as she tried to connect with her pack mate. Images flashed: *dark claws; sharp, snapping teeth; glowing blue and green eyes; her grandmother's horrified face*—

Something was attacking her house—and Gran!

Adriane bolted toward the cottage, half blinded by the terrifying images. Her wolf stone blazed with sharp pulses, its golden magic amplified by her fear.

"Gran?" Bursting through the cottage's open front door, she called out frantically, "Where are you?"

A ferocious snarling came from somewhere inside. Adriane raised her wolf stone, sending bands of gold flooding through the afternoon shadows.

"Adriane?"

Emily, Kara, Lyra, and Ozzie ran through the door.

"What's happening?" Emily asked.

"Something's in here," Adriane said quietly.

Kara and Emily instantly took fighting stances behind the warrior, jewels ready.

"Dreamer?" Adriane called out.

Her only reply was sharp static. But underneath she could feel the hunger, the driving bloodlust of the hunt.

The mages crept into the living room.

"No!" Adriane screamed.

Gran lay motionless on the living room floor, frail arms crossed as if trying to protect herself. And standing over her was Dreamer—teeth bared and feral.

Chapter 3

"**T**he doctors say a severe shock put Gran in a coma, but her condition is stable," Dr. Carolyn Fletcher, Emily's mom, explained, walking with Adriane, Emily, and Kara across the wide parking lot of Stonehill Hospital. "But Adriane, honey, she's also an elderly woman. It could be a stroke. These things happen."

"She's under some kind of spell," the healer said telepathically to Adriane and Kara.

"An enchantment," Kara added, blue eyes dark with contemplation as she twirled the unicorn jewel between two fingers.

Emily shook her head. *"My healing magic couldn't break it."*

"Where's Dreamer now?" Carolyn asked.

"He's with—" Kara started. They hadn't said anything about Dreamer being with Gran.

"He's at my house," Adriane quickly finished. "He's just a little upset."

"Upset?" Dr. Fletcher raised an eyebrow as she stopped at her green Explorer.

"He's fine now, really," Emily assured her mother.

Carolyn took a deep breath as she beeped open the SUV's door lock. "Now listen to me, girls. You know I support your efforts at the preserve."

The three mages stopped near the rear door and looked at one another.

"Uh-oh." Emily winced. *"Here it comes."*

"But it might be time to think about other plans," Carolyn said.

"Mom, can we discuss this at home—" Emily started.

Carolyn held up her hand—which meant, *Zip it, we discuss now.*

The mages climbed into the backseat, Emily and Kara flanking Adriane.

"What happened to your plans for expanding the Pet Palace, Em?" Carolyn asked, sliding into the driver's seat. "Not to mention school and band practice."

"Mom, you don't understand!"

"What? What don't I understand, Emily?" Carolyn asked, turning to her daughter. "The city council received a highly agitated call from your tour group."

"Dreamer didn't attack anyone, Dr. F.," Adriane insisted.

"They claim he did," Carolyn replied, starting the ignition. "There have been clear cases of wild animals turning on their handlers."

"Not Dreamer!" Adriane cried, wolf stone flaring.

As Carolyn pulled out of the parking lot, she glanced at the girls in the rearview mirror. "I know this is a lot to deal with right now," she said gently, "but perhaps it's time to think about placing Dreamer in a secure place."

"Like a zoo, or a circus?" Adriane cried. "No way!"

"Mom! That would be terrible!" Emily objected.

"I don't have to remind you of what we went through last summer," Carolyn continued. "Another wild animal getting loose is the last thing the town council wants to hear."

"It's a preserve—they're *supposed* to be loose," Adriane said.

"They see Dreamer as a potentially dangerous animal," Dr. Fletcher said. "I mean, no one even knows where he came from. If we don't do something, someone else will—and they might not have Dreamer's best interests at heart."

"Dreamer didn't attack anyone," Adriane protested again.

"He just wouldn't, Mom!"

"And I suppose he told you that?" Carolyn asked.

"He can't!" Adriane exclaimed, then caught herself. "Uh, I mean, we just know."

"You can't talk to him?" Emily asked.

Adriane tensed. *"Something's wrong with his magic."*

"Why didn't you tell us?" Kara locked eyes with Adriane.

"I dunno . . ." Noting the uncertain look Emily and

30

Kara exchanged, she added firmly, *"Dreamer was trying to protect Gran."*

"From what?" Kara asked, horrified at the revelation.

"Have any of you been listening to a word I've been saying?" Carolyn demanded.

"What did you say, Mom?"

"Adriane," Carolyn sighed, "what about moving in with Emily and me until Gran gets out of the hospital? You're family; we'd love to have you."

"Totally," Emily agreed.

"Thanks, Doctor F., but . . . ," Adriane began.

"I insist you move in with Emily," Kara said, looking from Adriane to Emily.

"I'd feel better at home."

"How about if Kara and I move in with Adriane?" Emily suggested.

"We have lots of food left over from the party," Kara said.

Dr. Fletcher nodded. "If Kara's parents agree, then it's a deal—at least for the weekend."

Emily and Kara leaned close to Adriane, their three jewels pulsing.

"Adriane, what is going on?" Emily asked.

"Something is on the preserve," Adriane said.

"What is it?" Kara asked. *"How come you and Dreamer are the only ones sensing it?"*

Carolyn's eyes darted to the rearview mirror. "You know, ever since you girls took over running the preserve, it's as if you've been hiding something, keeping a secret."

"That's so silly," Kara replied. *"Tonight, group meeting. Don't tell anyone!"*

❧   ❧   ❧

"Where's my other Elmo?" Ronif, a duck-like quiffle, wailed.

"RRRR!" Lyra growled. She had two moose slippers on back paws, one pink bunny on her left front, and an Elmo slipper on her right front paw.

"I'll trade you SpongeBob for the bunny," Balthazar, a pegasus, said, nodding to the mismatched set of slippers adorning his hooves.

The cottage's cozy living room was filled to capacity with mages, magical animals, and enough sleeping bags, blankets, and pillows for everyone.

Adriane sat curled on the oversized lounger, gently stroking Dreamer's back. The wolf lay at her feet, chin on his front paws, eyes anxiously darting over the room.

Whap!

A pair of red pajamas decorated with robots flew across the room, hitting Adriane in the head.

"Sleepover rule number one: Everyone wears pajamas!" Kara yelled, digging in her bulging suitcase, which she had opened in the middle of the Navajo patterned rug. All the animals swarmed around, picking out matching sleepwear.

"I prefer my sweats," Adriane said, eyeing Kara's pink satin sleeping set.

"Those are for Dreamer."

"Ooo, I'll take these." Emily reached into the suitcase and pulled out a pair of blue chenille socks that matched her moon-and-star-patterned flannel pajamas.

"Lyra, heads up." Kara sent a stuffed cat, monkey, and bear flying out of the overstuffed bag. "Everyone grab a snuggly."

Lyra deftly caught the snugglies and walked around distributing a mouthful to everyone.

Dreamer sat eye to eye with a snow-white rabbit with long, floppy ears.

"Ohhhhhhh," Tweek groaned miserably.

"That's not a very good place for you to rest, you know," Rasha, another quiffle, pointed out.

The twiggy elemental was lying flat in the fireplace.

"Popcorn's ready!" Ozzie tottered into the cottage's living room holding a huge bowl over his head. Maneuvering the maze of snugglies, he avoided tripping over the hem of his oversized plaid pj's.

"Yum!" Rasha stuck her beak in the bowl.

"That's disgusting!" Ozzie complained.

Emily helped Ozzie set the bowl on the long coffee table and grabbed a handful. She flopped on the couch next to the white owl so Ariel could snack, too.

Kara rolled her eyes as the animals crowded

around, grabbing wingfuls and pawfuls of hot popcorn.

Dreamer stayed where he was, head down, watching all the activity with wary liquid-green eyes.

"Time to call this meeting to order," Kara said, satisfied that all the animals had matching pairs of sleepwear. She strode to the center of the comfortable living room to address the group. "As you all know, today's opening tour spectacular was . . . not."

"It sucked," a baby quiffle squawked.

"Who's seen anything weird on the preserve?" Kara asked.

Everyone raised a hand, paw, wing, or flipper.

"I mean today."

All eyes turned to Adriane and Dreamer.

"Hey, this isn't a trial," Emily said, then turned to her friend. "So what's going on?"

"Spill it!" Kara ordered.

"Okay." Adriane scratched Dreamer's silky black ruff and tucked her long hair behind her ears. "Last night I had a really weird dream," she began. "I was running through Ravenswood and wound up in the magic glade, but everything was different."

"Go on," Emily urged gently.

"I was attacked."

"By what?" Kara asked.

Adriane took a deep breath. "A mistwolf."

A unified gasp filled the room.

"Inconceivable!" Tweek declared.

With a snarl, Dreamer thrashed his head back and forth. White fur flew in a frenzy as a rabbit ear went flying across the room. The wolf looked up, holding the remains of his snuggly between clenched jaws.

"You killed it!" Kara was appalled.

With a low whine, the wolf slunk back down, head lowered.

"Adriane, things always appear different in dreams," Emily pointed out.

"It wasn't a dream exactly." Adriane pushed up the leg of her sweats, revealing the ragged scratches. "There's more."

Silence fell across the warmly lit room.

Adriane shuddered with the memory. "In the glade I met a forest sylph called Orenda and then a mistwolf—"

"Rewind," Kara ordered. "What's a sylph?"

"It's an elemental fairy creature." Tweek wobbled across the rug. "Every magical forest has an earth sylph as a protector."

"Why haven't we seen it before?" Ozzie asked.

"You have, just not in its original form. A sylph melds into the forest, spreading magic." Tweek twirled toward Emily. "Didn't you tell me you found your jewels here?"

"I found mine in the lake," Emily explained. "Adriane found hers in the portal field."

"Well, I saw the sylph," the warrior murmured. "She was under attack also."

"By mistwolves?" Kara asked.

"No. Spiders."

Tweek's twigs poked out in astonishment.

"She was trapped in a huge spiderweb. It was awful. She was in terrible pain. And"—Adriane hung her head, trying to control her emotions—"there wasn't anything I could do to help her."

"Well, that doesn't sound good at all. What else?" Kara pressed.

"Nothing. Dreamer woke me, and Gran was sick," Adriane continued, taking a deep breath. "Gran said . . . the forest spirit was dying."

Everyone stared at Adriane and Dreamer.

"Why didn't you tell us?" Kara found her voice first.

"Do you tell me about every dream you have?" Adriane challenged.

"If I thought it was important, I would," Kara replied.

"Adriane, we're your friends," Emily said. "You're supposed to tell us."

Kara raised her arms in the air. "After all the work I did with the council, getting my dad to hook up the tour. Everything is in jeopardy!"

Adriane jumped to her feet, jewel pulsing. "Why is it always about you?"

Kara stepped back, caught off guard.

Dreamer sprang to the warrior's side, a low growl rising in his throat.

If Kara perceived any kind of threat, she didn't show it, dismissing the warrior with a flick of her wrist. "That's not what I meant. Hello! If we lose this tour, the council could shut down the whole place."

"You don't think I know that?" Adriane cried. "This is my home!"

"Well, I can't put a spin on all this bad publicity, no matter how good I am," Kara said.

"Oh, you'll figure something out." Adriane stalked across the rug, turning on Kara. "What Kara wants, Kara gets—right?"

The blazing star flushed, releasing a pulse of bright white from her jewel.

Lyra stepped to Kara's side, hackles raised.

The animals shuffled nervously, feeling the tension rising.

"Just go to Daddy, he'll fix it for you," Adriane taunted.

Emily stepped between her friends, but looked at the warrior. "Adriane, that's not fair."

Kara's face fell. "I'm not like that anymore."

Dreamer growled, teeth flashing in a wolf grin.

"You know, Adriane . . ." Kara faced the warrior. "You and I have been through a lot, and believe it or not, I understand how you feel."

"Kara, there is no way you can understand how I feel!" Adriane felt the room closing in. Her chest was tight, emotions raw. "You think it's so easy! You saved the Fairy Realms, bonded with a paladin, and—" She stopped abruptly.

"And what?" Kara's eyes squinted suspiciously.

"Nothing."

"I know what you were going to say."

"Leave me alone." Adriane whirled away, hair flying.

Kara pressed on. "You were going to say I saved Lyra, weren't you?"

"Get away from me!" Adriane's wolf stone sparked dangerously.

"And *you* couldn't save Storm!"

Adriane's jewel erupted with power.

"Adriane!" Emily shouted.

Kara's unicorn jewel flared bright. The two beams smacked together, diamond light against golden fire.

With a snarl, Dreamer lunged.

"Ahh!" Kara jumped back.

Lyra sprang in front of Kara. *"Calm your wolf down, now!"*

The two animals faced each other, teeth bared.

"That's enough!" Amplified by his ferret stone, Ozzie's voice boomed across the room. The ferret marched between the much larger animals and pushed them apart. "You should be ashamed of yourselves!"

"What's going on?" Emily asked in shock, running her healing jewel over Dreamer. "Adriane, I've never seen you like this."

Adriane fell on the couch. Dreamer moved to her feet, head lowered, tail between his legs.

Emily sat next to her friend. "Losing Storm has been really hard on you," she said gently. "And now with Gran—"

"Stop shrinking me!" Adriane cried, all her emotions bubbling to the surface. "I'm sorry. I don't know what's going on."

Storm had been her first real friend, and now she was gone. The thought of losing someone else she loved filled her with white-hot fear.

"It's okay, Adriane," Ozzie said, placing a paw on Adriane's hand.

"I don't know how, but I saw the forest spirit, and she told me she was sick." Adriane wiped her cheeks and sniffled. "But I was at the glade this morning, and there was nothing there. How did I see her?"

"World walking," the E. F. said, pulling his twigs together. "It means traveling through the astral planes. Mistwolves are the only living creatures who connect to the spirit world, and it's difficult for them."

"What are the astral planes, anyway?" Emily asked. "Are they connected to the magic web?"

"The magic web connects all physical worlds like Earth and Aldenmor," Tweek explained. "The astral planes lie hidden from the web, only intersecting in certain places. There are several layers, including the dream state, and on top of that, the spirit world."

"I've been there before," Kara said excitedly. "Lucinda brought me there."

"I doubt if you could go back by yourself. A human world walker is extremely rare—BlaH!" Tweek shuddered violently.

"What's wrong with you?" Kara asked.

"I'm feeling a bit scattered," Tweek groaned. "When mistwolves die, they join the spirit pack, giving their magic back to the living wolves."

"So it was the spirit pack I saw?" Adriane asked.

"Possibly."

"You miss Storm so much, you dreamed about a mistwolf," Kara said. "Case solved."

"But I *saw* it. It was a ghost. And I think it attacked Gran."

"This is the real world," Emily said, unconvinced. "There are no such things as ghosts."

"*There's one,*" Ariel reported, perched on the windowsill.

The mages and animals scrambled over to the window.

Outside, a twinkling light bobbed gently up and down. With a soft flash, the light was suddenly inside the living room.

"What is that?" Ozzie asked, sparkly bits tickling his whiskers.

A small winged creature spun around Tweek, checking him out. Lights ran around its body, pulsing from delicate wings.

"Looks like Tinkerbell," Emily said.

"It's a fairy wraith," Kara exclaimed, holding out her finger so the tiny fairy creature could land upon it. "They loved me in the Fairy Realms."

But the small fairy was not interested in Kara.

With a tinkling of bells, the wraith zipped to Adriane, flashing brightly.

Adriane heard something familiar. The wraith's bells carried a fragment of Orenda's song, the song of the forest.

Suddenly the wraith zipped back out the window, hovering in the air expectantly.

"A Ravenswood fairy wraith," Tweek gasped. "Follow it!"

"Let's go," Adriane said as the light sped off into the woods.

Dreamer howled in agreement, scrambling anxiously toward the cottage's front door.

"Everyone stay here!" Kara ordered as Balthazar barreled past her. "You'll ruin your slippers!"

"It's headed toward the manor house," Emily pointed out, digging for her jacket in the pile of blankets and pillows.

Adriane slipped into her parka vest and stepped outside into the chilly night. It was unusually cold for spring, making her breath cloud in front of her.

Dreamer ran after the glittering trail of fairy dust winding through the dark woods.

Adriane's heart raced as she followed the wolf

along the cobblestone path that led from her house. This felt eerily like her dream, following a mysterious summons through the shadowy forest.

"Wait up, Tink," Kara called to the fairy wraith, as she, Emily, and Lyra hurried through the trees to the main driveway.

The manor house loomed in the night, dark and imposing. Moonlight glinted off the high turrets and peaked roofs. The wraith streaked up the front steps—and vanished.

The mages hurried up the steps, casting beams of jewel light over the large double doors.

Suddenly, the front door creaked open.

Three girls, a ferret, an owl, a cat, a wolf, and a pile of twigs peered into the dark foyer.

The wraith wavered and zipped down the hallway.

The group slowly moved after it.

"It's in the kitchen," Emily whispered.

The light bounced across shiny polished pots and pans hanging from the ceiling, then off the heavy steel of the double freezer before zipping through a wooden door.

Ozzie, Tweek, and Ariel slowly pushed the door open. In front of them, a circular staircase spiraled down into blackness.

"Tink's leading us to the basement," Adriane exclaimed.

"But why?" Kara wondered. "There's just old stuff down there."

"That's the only kind of stuff in this house," Ozzie commented.

"Let's go!" Kara ordered, then stepped out of Lyra's way. "After you."

Creeping down the stairs, the group followed Lyra and Dreamer through corridors stacked with piles of old furniture, lawn chairs, and broken statues.

The mysterious wraith was bobbing in front of them, softly blinking, as if checking to make sure they were all there. It floated into a dusty room filled with metal racks crowded with cardboard file boxes, old crates, and dusty knickknacks.

Suddenly the light vanished.

"Where did it go?" Ozzie asked.

Jewel light pierced the darkness, crisscrossing the room.

"Spread out, there must be a secret panel or door," Kara instructed.

The mages separated, moving down different corridors.

Adriane's head pounded—she felt disoriented, the dark corridor blurring before her eyes. Dreamer stood close, his muscles tense. Something was definitely down here.

"Emily, you see anything?" the warrior asked anxiously.

"Nope," Emily answered, then called out. "Ozzie?"

"Nope, Tweek?"

"I'm standing right next to you!"

"Gah. Kara?"

"Kara?" Emily called again after a few seconds. But there was no answer.

"She's gone!" Lyra growled, padding to the wall, sniffing.

"Kara!" Everyone called out.

"Mmhphfff." Something was making a racket, from *behind* the wall. "Getttmmmmeeeeouttt!"

Tweek and Ozzie scrambled up an old dusty chair, climbing onto a ledge above Adriane.

"Kara, is that you?" Ozzie asked, knocking on the wall.

A horrible shriek echoed from the other side.

"It's her," Adriane confirmed, running her hands over the ledge on the wall. She felt a small trigger and pushed.

The wall suddenly slid open, revealing a terrified Kara.

"Good work," Tweek said.

But all Kara could do was point to the startling apparition behind her.

Adriane gasped as she stared into the snarling face of a glowing, silver mistwolf. Stormbringer.

Chapter 4

Ozzie screamed.

The ghostly figure of Stormbringer stepped forward, silvery outline shimmering.

"Storm?" Adriane whispered, wolf stone flashing. "Is it really you?"

"Pardon me." Tweek casually walked past the girls and right through the glowing ghost. The little elemental stopped in the belly of the wolf.

"Gah!" Ozzie grabbed his ears.

Tweek examined the image with his turquoise gemstone. "It's a cohesive light structure."

"A hologram," Emily realized, lowering her rainbow stone. She stepped forward and passed her hand through the image.

"I knew that," Ozzie said, nonchalantly smoothing his fur back in place.

Disappointment flooded through Adriane. Of course Storm wouldn't be here. Her pack mate was dead.

"See her feet and ears?" Emily pointed to the hologram.

"It's a younger Storm." Adriane looked closer. "About Dreamer's age."

"What is this place?" Kara strode into the large room, Lyra close by her side.

Dozens of candelabras abruptly flared to life, illuminating an immense cluttered room.

A table strewn with papers stood by the far wall. Enclosed glass shelves were crammed full of amulets, charms, and vials.

"Looks like a workroom." Emily was awed.

Lyra sniffed the air. *No one has been in here for years.*

"You!" Ozzie cried as the wraith materialized in front of his nose, waving her tiny hands.

The wraith dove under a pile of papers on the desk. Rifling and rummaging, she emitted a worried, high-pitched humming.

Ozzie scampered after her, sending papers flying. "Come back here!"

The wraith darted to the other side of the room, diving under Lyra's belly and leaving a trail of blue and violet twinkles.

"Here's the hologram's source." Using his gem like a magnifying glass, Tweek followed a thin beam of light to a crystal, set in a strange metallic device on the table. He lifted the crystal out, causing the wolf to appear and disappear. "This is a data crystal, the same design as my HORARFF."

Tweek was referring to the jewel that hung from his neck, his *Handbook of Rules and Regulations for Fairimentals*.

Adriane stepped over Ozzie. "Could there be any more images stored in it?"

The E. F. reset the crystal. "The image was stuck, but I should be able to—"

Suddenly Storm's hologram flashed, dissolving into another image: the forests of Ravenswood. The picture shifted over to a silver wolf pup playing in the field.

"This may be the only record of the last living mistwolf," a disembodied voice floated from the crystal.

"That voice," Kara exclaimed.

"It's Mr. Gardener!" Adriane gasped, stepping closer. Her wolf stone sparked as she watched Storm, so young and full of promise.

The voice of Gardener continued: "After I lost my wolf, I thought I would never see another again."

"Gardener was bonded to a mistwolf?" Ozzie asked.

"Hoo noo," Ariel cooed.

"This is big," Kara confirmed.

"Shhh!" Adriane whispered.

The images of Storm continued to play.

"I don't know where Stormbringer came from. It's as if she just appeared from the forests. I thought she could help me understand what happened, but she has no recollection of the other mistwolves and will not leave this place. It's as if she's waiting for something."

"Someone," Adriane breathed, wiping tears from her eyes.

"I know Storm is the one who can save the pack. I have betrayed them. I can no longer stay at Ravenswood."

The image abruptly cut off.

Adriane was totally stunned. Mr. Gardener had been right about one thing: Storm *had* saved the mistwolves. But she should have lived to see the pack flourish, should have spent a long life with Adriane, mage and bonded animal exploring their magic together. But Adriane had let her die—

Dreamer was at her side, wet nose nudging her hand as he whined with concern.

No. She still had a mistwolf to save.

"Did you have any idea?" Emily asked Adriane.

Adriane shook her head "Gardener was already gone when I got here."

"Something happened between Gardener and his wolf," Kara said.

Just like something had happened to Storm, Adriane thought. And now Dreamer. When humans bonded with mistwolves, did it always end in disaster? Is that why Tink had brought them here? Could

Storm be trying to reach her now? A ghostly presence from beyond—

Oooooooo.

"What was that?" Kara spun around, jewel sparking.

Ozzie lay on a stack of flat objects, Tink scratching his tummy. With a sigh, the ferret slid to the floor. Then he looked up to see everyone staring at him. He jumped to his feet. "What?"

The wraith squealed, happily somersaulting in the air.

"Hey, look at this." Ozzie turned over the wooden board he'd been lying on. "It looks like a secret code."

"It's a Ouija board, Ozzie," Emily said, examining the exquisite board engraved with bright red letters and numbers. There was a sparkling jewel in each of the four corners, mounted atop different painted designs. YES and NO were printed in the bottom corners.

"Everyone's seen those in horror movies," Kara explained. "You use them to contact spirits and ghosts."

"No way," Ozzie scoffed.

"Way," the blazing star nodded. "The spirit channels through someone and moves a wooden pointer over the board, spelling out messages."

"Here's the pointer." Emily held up a beautifully carved triangle with a large clear crystal in the center. She set it on the board.

"Wait! There are some very important rules you

49

have to follow," Kara warned. She held up her hand and counted off. "One, never go into a haunted house—especially after dark. Two, never, *ever*, go into the basement."

"So far, so good," Emily observed wryly. "We've already broken both."

"Oh," Kara continued in a hushed voice. "If the board spells out 'help me,' it always means there's a monster right behind you."

Ozzie whirled around, then jumped back.

Emily dragged a small chest to the middle of the room and set the board on top.

The mages, Tweek, and Ozzie crammed in, sitting cross-legged on the floor around the board. Lyra, Dreamer, and Ariel looked on.

"Okay, everyone: Paws, hands, and twigs on the pointer," Kara directed.

"Ask it a question," Adriane said.

"Can I buy a vowel?" Ozzie asked, surveying the graphic capital letters.

"Oooh, I know!" Kara exclaimed. She paused and cleared her throat, looking around the room with wide blue eyes. "What kind of quiz is Mrs. Herring giving in homeroom?"

The pointer didn't budge.

"Let's try to use our jewels," Emily suggested.

The mages, Fairimental, and ferret closed their eyes in concentration, breathing deeply. Amber, pink, blue, turquoise, and gold light filled the room.

"Is there a spirit in the house?" Emily asked in a hushed tone.

Instantly, an icy gust of wind extinguished the candles, plunging the room into darkness.

"Is that a yes?" Adriane asked.

Crrrreeeeeak! The door slammed shut, making everyone jump.

"Allrighty then," Kara said nervously. "Someone ask something."

"Storm, is that you?" Adriane whispered, peering around the room.

The jewel in the pointer started to glow, casting light across the board.

"Ooo." Ariel's big owl eyes opened wide.

"It's moving!" Kara squealed.

The pointer gently vibrated beneath their fingers, moving to the No.

"Are you Orenda?" Adriane asked, resting her fingers lightly on the pointer.

The pointer started blinking more brightly as it shifted and moved across the board to the Yes.

Suddenly the jewel blinked and started shaking.

"Stop shaking, Ozzie!" Adriane scolded.

"I'm not doing anything!" the frightened ferret protested.

Dreamer growled and paced up and down, his emerald eyes alert.

The pointer slid across the board, pausing on a series of letters until it had spelled out:

"This is bad," Kara said, and looked around the room, waiting for the monster to come crashing in.

"How can we help you?" Emily asked.

The pointer flew in zigzag patterns, spelling out another word:

STORM

Adriane's heart pounded. "How do we help Storm?"

The pointer turned bloodred. A sudden wail pierced the room.

"Tink!" Ozzie cried.

The little fairy stretched thin like a rubber band. Her glowing form winked in and out before vanishing in a puff of gold twinkles.

Adriane tried desperately to focus, but the room was spinning, making her dizzy.

"Whoa." Kara grabbed Lyra as the room suddenly started shaking before coming to an abrupt stop.

"That's not Orenda," Adriane said.

The pointer pulsed red like a heartbeat.

"Then who is it?" Ozzie asked.

"Blah!" Tweek shuddered and twitched.

"Who?"

The pointer flashed as the red light zipped into Tweek, sending his twiggy body whirling.

Tweek screamed, his voice deep and raspy. He rattled, twigs jerking and crunching. Suddenly he snapped back to normal. "Fascinating," he declared.

The E. F. spun in a circle, leaped in the air, and landed in a pile. "Chew on this!" he roared, quartz eyes flashing red, spitting loose twigs everywhere.

"What's happening to you, Tweek?" Emily asked.

"Interesting." Seemingly back to normal, Tweek blinked his quartz eyes. "I've been possessed by unspeakable evil."

Suddenly Tweek's limbs coiled, cracking as red eyes glowed malevolently from his distorted face. "I think . . ." His voice warped into a bone-chilling shriek. "Ravenswood will be destroyed!"

Tweek shuddered violently as he exploded in a flurry of twigs and vanished.

Chapter 5

Adriane walked briskly between the towering firs at the glade's edge. The morning sun glinted through leaves varnished with an emerald sheen by the night's rain. Bushes and ferns swayed, leaving trails of light dancing across small pools of water.

Reaching out with her wolf senses, the warrior tried to feel the presence of Orenda. "Spirit of Ravenswood, are you there?"

Orenda and Storm were both in trouble—somehow they were both connected.

She felt the sudden sting of awareness, as if she were being watched.

Adriane shivered. For the first time since coming to Ravenswood eighteen months ago, the forests felt cold, distant. Was it only the wind? Or something darker, hiding in the shadows.

A growl interrupted her dark thoughts. Dreamer's nose was in a bush, sniffing at something.

Adriane studied her pack mate. The wolf was tall and graceful; his puppy fat had tightened into rippling muscles. Lustrous jet-black fur marked with white paws and a star upon his chest gleamed like velvet. He was awesome.

She trained her senses on him, trying to connect. Jumbled images raced through her head—*gleaming spiderwebs trapping a monstrous figure with blazing red eyes*—

Adriane gasped. Had the mistwolf really seen the spiderwebs? Maybe she and Dreamer were just out of sync, freaked by her strange dream. Or maybe she *had* been world walking, like Tweek had suggested. And the danger only existed in the spirit world—for now.

Adriane focused harder, forcing a connection. Her jewel flashed and Dreamer stopped abruptly, shaking his head with a yowl of pain.

She drew back immediately. "Sorry."

Dreamer locked his deep green eyes on hers. The wolf stone pulsed, and fear tingled along her arms. His magic was slipping away. She turned, casting magic fire from her wrist. With a quick movement, she swirled the fire into a lasso, an easy exercise she had done hundreds of times. But the golden circle flared and fell apart, dissipating to sparks.

Adriane closed her eyes. What was happening? Was she losing the connection to her magic as well?

Tough it out, she told herself. All her life she had toughed it out.

Growing up, she'd moved around too much to make friends. She had always been the strange new girl. She was used to being alone, and it was easier that way.

Stormbringer had been her first true friend. The wolf had opened a whole new world to Adriane. But it wasn't just the magic that filled her with the sense of belonging she so desperately needed. It was also meeting Emily, Ozzie, Lyra—and even Kara. Without Storm, Adriane might never have met the most important people in her life—friends who loved her.

But now Storm was gone. She had not bonded with Dreamer like she had with Storm, and maybe she never would. When Storm died, a piece of Adriane had died with her, and the hole in her heart could not be filled with another.

A cloud passed over the sun, plunging the shimmering forest into shadows.

Dreamer followed her across the Mist Trail and into the open ground behind the cottage house. Gran had made it a real home for her and Adriane. It was always warm and welcoming, with delicious scents coming from the kitchen where Gran spent hours cooking. The responsibility of looking after the preserve must have been overwhelming, even for a woman of such determination and grit as Gran. Now it was up to Adriane. This was her home. Not only the stone and wood house, but also the hundreds of acres of forest preserve itself. And it could all be lost.

Adriane walked by a line of quiffles and brimbees stretching from her house practically to Wolf Run

Pass. The animals edged away anxiously as if they were scared of Dreamer—or of her.

The wolf kept his head low, following Adriane as she stepped onto the front porch. "What's this, the chow line?"

"Pre-tour inspection," Emily answered from the open kitchen window.

"Dear Fairimentals," Kara sang as she walked out the front door. She carried a bright silver case. "Need help. Tweek has exploded—again. Oh, and I got an A in Math!"

Adriane stared wide-eyed. Had Kara gone nuts?

"Message for the Fairimentals," Kara explained, allowing a hint of worry in her voice. "As soon as I can get through to Goldie, she can take it."

"No luck yet, huh?"

"No." Kara smiled weakly.

Adriane understood Kara's concern. The blazing star had formed a deep attachment to the mini dragon, and vice versa. The dragonflies could usually get through all kinds of magical interference, but if they couldn't even hear Kara . . . the mages would be completely on their own.

"In the meantime . . . ," Kara said, observing the long line of animals. She set the case on the porch's swinging bench. "I want everyone looking their best for today's tour."

Dreamer shifted restlessly, then lay down next to Lyra.

"You first, Dreamer," Kara said, popping open the silver case.

A golden clamshell mirror, jade brush, silver comb, powder puff, and skunk-shaped atomizer tumbled out excitedly.

"Quiet, quiet!" The silver comb clapped his feet. "Let the princess speak."

"Special assignment." Kara pointed to Lyra, Dreamer, and the line of quiffles, jeeran, and brimbees spilling off the front porch.

"Oooo! Mistwolf!" Skirmish, the jade brush, dove under Dreamer's tummy, making him leap to his feet.

"He stinks!" Whiffle scuttled toward Dreamer on crystal feet, puffing clouds of rose-scented perfume.

Dreamer took one sniff and sneezed.

"I'll just groom him myself, thank you very much." Adriane ran her own brush over Dreamer's silky fur before Puffdoggie, the powder puff, could unleash a cloud of sparkly powder.

"Princess Lyra's turn," Kara directed.

"Yay!" The enchanted objects dove into Lyra's orange-spotted fur.

"My fur needs to be extra shiny!" The large cat primped and preened with every stroke, brush, and spritz.

"I swear, Lyra, you're becoming more like Kara every day," Emily said as she walked through the sliding-screen door.

"Thank you."

Adriane turned away as the blazing star beamed at her bonded cat.

Emily knelt in front of Dreamer. Gently holding his head, she looked into his deep green eyes.

"What is it, Dreamer?" Emily's gem pulsed soft greens and blues. "What's wrong?"

The wolf cocked his head, leaned forward, and licked Emily on the nose.

The healer got to her feet with a sigh. "His magic is blocked."

"It's like he's lost," Adriane said softly, glancing at her gem. The paw-shaped stone lay quietly on her black and turquoise bracelet.

"No." Emily firmly faced the warrior. "Not while he has you."

"I can't help him!" Adriane cried, her voice cracking with emotion. She knelt next to her pack mate, hugging him protectively.

The others waited, staring as she took a deep breath.

"Something is here." Adriane gently stroked the wolf under his chin, turning his liquid green eyes to her own. "It's doing something to Dreamer." She was about to add *and to me.*

"We've searched the whole preserve," Kara said. "No one has seen anything."

"Then it's something we can't see," Emily stated.

"How do we fight something we can't even see?" Kara asked.

"We just haven't figured out how to look," Adriane said, rising to her feet.

"No bows!" Lyra growled as the accessories attempted to secure a scented purple ribbon around the cat's neck.

Mirabelle, the clamshell mirror, flapped open, releasing a gob of green liquid that settled over the quiffle's head feathers.

"Cool," Rasha said, admiring Ronif's new coif. "What is it?"

"Duckity doo."

"What about us?"

The animals surged forward onto the porch, crowding the mages.

"One at a time," Emily shouted. "Kara, I think your accessories may be a bit overkill—Kara?"

The blazing star was gazing through the oak trees that arched over Adriane's cobbled walkway.

"Heads up," Kara said, pointing to the circular driveway in front of the manor house. "We've got company." A line of cars was making its way down the main road toward Ravenswood Manor.

Kara consulted her watch. "The tour isn't supposed to be here for two more hours."

Dreamer sprang to his feet, a low growl rumbling in his throat.

"Adriane, take Dreamer to the glade." Emily's face was tight with concern. "Now."

"Pancakes are ready!" Ozzie ran from the kitchen, blobs of whipped cream flying off his fur.

"Let's go!" Balthazar shouted, herding the magical animals off the porch and into the forest behind the cottage.

"Dreamer, come on." Adriane's jewel sparked as she saw the dark SUV screeching to a stop in the circular driveway. It was followed by a patrol car marked with the Stonehill sheriff star.

The wolf hunched low, growling and snapping at the air before taking off for the trees.

"Dreamer!" Adriane yelled.

"I'll go after him." Lyra bounded off the porch, vanishing into the forest.

"Is it the good witch or the bad witch?" Kara asked, frowning.

The SUV's door swung open, and a stout gray-haired woman stepped out. Beasley Windor's steely eyes darted everywhere at once as she marched toward the cottage.

"What's *she* doing here?" Ozzie asked.

"She's brought Sheriff Nelson," Emily said nervously, watching the angry city council woman approach with the sheriff.

Kara stepped forward. "I'll handle this."

"Good morning, Mrs. Windor." Kara flashed her diamond bright smile. "Hello, Sheriff Nelson."

"Hi, Kara," the sheriff smiled. "How're you doing?"

"I'm terrific. You get the brownies we sent over?"

"We sure did. Your mom bakes them really swell—"

Windor cut him off with an icy stare.

"Sorry, Kara," Sheriff Nelson whispered. "We're here on business."

"We have all our permits," Kara said. "I made sure they were filed—"

"Do you have a permit for—*this!*" Mrs. Windor shouted, holding up the *Stonehill Gazette*.

Bold letters jumped out on the front page: **"WOLF ATTACK AT RAVENSWOOD PRE-SERVE!"** Below the headline was a full-color photo of the horrified tourists.

"That was an accident," Kara said calmly. "No one was hurt."

"I'm afraid it's gone beyond that, Kara," the sheriff said.

"These wild animals have terrorized the town long enough," Mrs. Windor snapped. "We've come for the wolf."

"He didn't do anything!" Adriane protested. Her jewel pulsed a warning.

"Adriane." Emily held her friend's arm.

"What do you know about taking care of animals?" Adriane cried, wrestling away from Emily to get in Mrs. Windor's face.

"Enough to realize you have no business running

this preserve," Mrs. Windor responded, staring the warrior in the eye. "And now it's over."

Adriane blinked. For a split second, Mrs. Windor's eyes had flashed red.

Kara pulled Adriane back. "My father gave us full authority to watch over these animals."

"Who do you think authorized the sheriff's visit, Missy?"

The sheriff nodded. "Sorry, Kara. We have our orders."

"I'm calling him right now." Kara whipped out her pink cell phone and hit the speed dial.

"Mrs. Windor," Emily said, trying to remain calm. "We have a tour in an hour—it's very important we have all our animals here."

"The tours are all canceled," the city council woman stated, holding the newspaper. "There will be no tour today, or ever."

"I need to talk to my father right now!" Kara screamed into her phone.

Fear gnawed at Adriane's stomach as a plume of dust rose on the main road. Another vehicle pulled up to the manor.

"You can't do this," Adriane hissed.

Beasley Windor smiled wickedly. "Just watch me."

"My mother will straighten this out," Emily said as Dr. Fletcher's green Explorer pulled to a stop.

The vet stepped out the driver's door, followed by two other people in the back.

"Oh, no." Adriane turned ashen.

"Who are they?" Emily whispered to Adriane as the trio approached.

Adriane stepped back. "My parents."

"Adriane." A tall, athletic man strode past Mrs. Windor to stand in front of Adriane. He wore loose blue jeans and a dark blue blazer over a white T-shirt. Brown eyes shone from a ruggedly handsome face framed by long brown wavy hair.

"What are you doing here?" Adriane asked in disbelief.

He stopped and smiled awkwardly. A slightly built, dark-haired woman approached hesitantly behind him. Her olive skin set off intense black eyes.

"How long did you expect us to wait until you called, Adriane?" her mother asked.

"We just came from the hospital," Adriane's father said in a slight French accent. "Your grandmother's condition is unchanged."

Adriane's mother put her hand on her daughter's cheek, a tiny smile fleeting across her pretty features.

Adriane was surprised to find herself standing a little taller than her mother.

Her dad turned his attention to Mrs. Windor and the sheriff. "I'm Luc Charday, and this is my wife, Willow."

"Beasley Windor, Stonehill city council." Mrs. Windor nodded curtly. "Your daughter and her friends have been keeping dangerous animals on this preserve and jeopardizing the entire town," she accused.

"She doesn't know what she's talking about!" Adriane cried furiously. "Dreamer didn't do anything!"

"Dreamer?" Willow asked, her eyes full of concern.

"It's a wild wolf," Windor broke in.

"He's not wild!" Adriane rounded angrily on the stout woman.

Suddenly a howl echoed from the trees.

Willow's long dark hair fell over her black eyes as she anxiously took in the preserve.

"No!" Adriane shouted. "Stay away!"

But it was no use. Responding to his pack mate's distress, Dreamer lunged from the trees, landing between Adriane and Mrs. Windor. He looked fierce and ready to strike.

Emily dashed to the snarling mistwolf, pulling him back.

"You see that?" Windor scrambled behind the sheriff. "That wolf attacked me!"

Luc eyed the big black wolf. "Adriane, this isn't exactly a golden retriever."

"You don't even know him," Adriane shot back, stepping in front of her pack mate.

"Mom!" Emily pleaded.

"We went over this," Dr. Fletcher said evenly. "The animal needs to be in a safe environment."

"We've come to take you back with us," Willow said quietly to Adriane.

"You just show up out of nowhere and expect me to leave? Ravenswood is my home!"

"Adriane, we want—" Luc began, but stopped short as a large yellow and brown van pulled up behind the sheriff's car. Wire mesh covered the rear windows.

Adriane gasped as she read the logo on the van's side: DEPARTMENT OF FISH AND GAME.

"You can't do this!" Adriane grabbed Dreamer in a fierce hug. "You can't take him away from me!"

Two men in tan uniforms jumped out, carrying nets and rifles.

"Why did you even come here?" Adriane cried. Red-hot fear spiked through her. "I hate you for this!"

Willow cringed.

"Mom!" Emily begged.

"Dad!" Kara wailed into her cell.

"Dreamer, run!" Adriane cried, trying to push the wolf from the porch.

"Pack mates stand together," the mistwolf insisted, hackles raised as he stood his ground.

For a second, Adriane was startled—Dreamer had spoken.

"Adriane," Luc said, pulling her away from the wolf. "We'll figure something out. Just let the sheriff do his job."

"He won't feel a thing." One of the game wardens cocked a tranq gun, leveling it at Dreamer.

She heard Emily yell, *"Kara, no!"* as the blazing star raised her jewel.

"Turn to mist!" Adriane screamed, trying to break free of her father's strong grasp. *"Please! They won't hurt me."*

Dreamer pawed the ground, unsure what to do. His eyes fixed on his pack mate as the men closed in. Adriane reached out, trying desperately to help him. She felt his magic at the edges of her mind, but it was ragged and broken. He couldn't turn to mist.

Flashes of Storm's golden eyes played through her mind, flooding pain through her until she could barely breathe. This couldn't be happening to her, not again!

"Pack mate!"

With a wild snarl, Dreamer lunged.

"Look out!" the sheriff shouted.

Two loud bangs cracked through the still air.

Dreamer howled as the yellow darts sank deep into his side.

"No!" Adriane broke away from her father and ran toward her pack mate.

The wolf fell into Adriane's arms, struggling as the tranquilizer took hold.

"Stay with me," she pleaded, burying her face in his silky fur.

Dulled emerald eyes focused on her as he tried to stay conscious.

Adriane was suddenly pulled to her feet, torn away from the drugged wolf.

"Adriane, let him go," Luc said.

"How can you let them do this?" Adriane shouted wildly, pushing away from her parents, tears streaming down her face.

The warrior watched helplessly as a heavy net tightened over the wolf.

"Do you have to do that?" Emily shouted angrily. "He's got enough tranq to knock out an animal twice his size!"

"He won't be causing trouble again," Mrs. Windor said, watching with satisfaction.

"We're going to get him back," Emily promised.

"I'll convince my dad," Kara said, running to Adriane's side.

"*Dreamer!*" the warrior called frantically, her wolf stone pulsing bright gold. "*Dreamer, are you all right?*"

But the unconscious mistwolf could not answer.

"No!" A primal cry ripped from Adriane's throat as the officers tossed Dreamer's limp body into the back of the van and shut the doors, blocking him from sight.

For the second time, she had failed her pack mate.

Chapter 6

The Dark Sorceress descended a staircase deep beneath the lair. The stone closed around her like a crypt. "How long must I be confined to this dank place?" she snarled.

To the sorceress's surprise, the Spider Witch cackled, an ugly screeching sound.

"You would prefer the void of the Otherworlds?"

Crystals embedded in the walls cast dull yellow light, illuminating the Spider Witch's bulky form as they moved along a corridor.

The sorceress shuddered. She hated the nothingness of the Otherworlds, but this was getting intolerable. Now, finally free, the craving for magic made her blood pulse fever hot. How much longer could she watch this witch cast weaving spells and not be able to use magic herself?

The Dark Sorceress's animal eyes focused on dozens of faded tapestries lining the walls. They were all nearly identical to the Ravenswood scene the spiders were now weaving.

"You have tried this before." The sorceress ran her

hands over a frayed image of the imposing manor house. "What makes you think you will succeed this time?"

"The wizard who guarded Ravenswood is gone," the witch snapped. "This time, *I* will control the magic of Ravenswood."

The sorceress frowned as she passed more decaying tapestries. "We need to retrieve the remaining power crystals."

"Precisely." The witch turned insect eyes on the sorceress. "I believe one has landed in the astral planes."

The sorceress stopped short. She had used the elusive planes to focus her dream magic, but it was exhausting and unreliable. What was the witch planning? It would be impossible to enter the astral planes, let alone bring back something solid like a power crystal. "And just how do you propose to get to the astral planes?"

"You know very well there is one creature capable of walking the spirit trail."

Mistwolves!

The sorceress flushed with anger. She had come so close to stealing the magic of the mistwolves. She would have succeeded if not for the warrior and her wolf.

Sensing the sorceress's thoughts, the Spider Witch sneered. "Where you failed, I will succeed." She gathered her robes and swiftly moved through an arched doorway.

The Dark Sorceress followed, brushing stray spiderwebs from her pale cheek. She stepped into a large chamber.

An enormous glowing tapestry stretched from floor to ceiling, radiating power. Silvers, blues, greens, and reds looped and twisted in complicated patterns, like interlocking dreamcatchers amid a dazzling array of stars. It was a map of the magic web.

"How is this possible?" Stunned, the sorceress forced her voice to remain steady. "Even a fairy map contains only a small section of the web—it is impossible to map the entire thing."

"At the core, it is a just a web, a pattern of magic," the witch said smugly. "But you are right: This is not the magic web."

The Dark Sorceress breathed a sigh of relief. The thought of her ally having that kind of power was terrifying.

"It is a new design," the Spider Witch laughed.

The sorceress contained herself. "You would need all nine power crystals to control the magic of Avalon. But the Fairimentals guard two, and the blazing star destroyed a third."

"You would need all nine to maintain the web as it is," the witch replied, indicating four brightly glowing points on the map. "By controlling each of these key places, I can harness enough wild magic to re-weave the web. One that I will control."

The sorceress listened with mounting concern.

"You see this point?" the witch said, running her hands along the tapestry, pausing on a bright pulsing point. "It is this lair."

"Ravenswood is another point," the sorceress surmised. So the Spider Witch already controlled one of four points, and was trying to capture Ravenswood as well.

"The third is on Aldenmor," the witch continued, indicating another glowing light. "But you know that." Insect eyes stared, cold and lifeless.

Aldenmor, the heart of the Fairimentals.

The fourth point pulsed erratically and disappeared, then flared again on the opposite side of the pattern.

"The fourth is most elusive. Its location changes—floating hidden among the swirling strands of the web." The witch shrugged dismissively.

"You still have to find Avalon itself," the Dark Sorceress insisted. "It is the source of all magic."

"Once I re-weave the web, Avalon will be revealed."

The sorceress stood back, the enormity of the witch's master plan sinking in. Twisting the magic of Ravenswood made the warrior weak, while strengthening the demon. The demon would create enough chaos on the astral planes to attract the power crystal where a mistwolf would retrieve it.

It was brilliant.

And horrifying.

There would be no place for the sorceress in the web's new design.

"Yes, this is certainly quite a surprise," the sorceress said softly.

The Spider Witch laughed. "The last surprise of the mages' lives."

❧　　❧　　❧

"This is awful!" Ozzie cried, stumbling over a pile of sneakers as he followed Adriane into her closet.

"You should see Kara's room," Lyra said, nosing a loose soccer ball as she followed the ferret.

"No, I mean Adriane can't leave!" the ferret protested. "I was sent here to find three mages."

"And you did." The warrior pulled her long hair into a ponytail. Gently lifting Ariel's foot, she thumbed through several hangers.

"Well, this isn't a temporary position." Ozzie climbed up the chest of drawers to stare at the dark-haired girl.

Adriane stood nose to noses as the ferret, cat, and owl pressed forward in the cramped closet. "I don't have much time."

She grabbed a black vest and slipped by the animals. The wall behind her bed was plastered with posters of rock musicians and snowboarders. Part of another wall had been painted with stars and flying comets. Carved blocks of painted cedar littered a table, folk art sculptures she had started. She hadn't gotten around to finishing her projects—it didn't seem to matter much now.

Ariel took wing, turquoise and aqua sparkles running through her feathers as she landed on the headboard. "Hoono!"

"I'm not leaving just yet." Adriane belted her black jeans and tied her boots tight.

"Then what are you doing?" the ferret demanded, ducking as Lyra stretched her lithe body across the rug.

The warrior regarded the three animals, her gem sparkling with contained fire. "Something is out there, and I'm going to find it."

"All right. Let's go." Lyra stood, and her sleek muscles rippled under lustrous orange fur.

"Hookay," Ariel agreed, blue eyes blinking.

"I'm going alone."

"Gah! Does Emily know about this?" Ozzie asked, shuffling back and forth.

"No, and you are not going to say anything!" The determination in Adriane's voice left no room for argument.

The animals exchanged glances.

Ozzie started pacing. "You're going to try that world walking stuff again, aren't you?"

"Listen to me," she said, sighing, the corners of her mouth lifting into a smile. "I love you guys."

She gently smoothed down Ariel's head feather as

Lyra rubbed against the warrior's side. "But you can't come with me. You have to trust me on this one."

The three animals silently stared back.

"If I get into trouble, I'll call you, Ozzie. Okay?"

"All right," Ozzie reluctantly agreed, ferret stone flashing on his collar. "But I don't like it one bit."

Ferret, cat, and owl exchanged a nod.

"Remember," Ozzie added. "I'm just a stone call away."

Adriane hurried down the stairs. She had to move quickly. Kara and Emily were busy with school projects and chores, and her parents had gone back to the hospital to check on Gran. But everyone would return soon enough.

Stepping out the back door, she breathed in the cool evening air. The setting sun wrapped the forest in shimmering golden light. Hurrying into the deepening shadows of the trees, she made her way to the immense Rocking Stone, jutting into the sky like an accusing finger.

She hadn't told Ozzie, Lyra, and Ariel all she intended to do tonight.

Focusing on the warm golden glow of her jewel, she cleared her mind and concentrated. She wasn't completely sure how to go world walking, but she had been on the spirit trail once before. She had run with Storm on the ancient mistwolf stream of consciousness when the spirit pack helped her heal Dreamer. Adriane had been able to reach Storm across any distance—even across time and space itself. Could she reach her first pack mate again?

Before she even entered the glade, Adriane felt the sickness seeping into the fabric of the forest.

She reached with her wolf senses, something that had always come so naturally to her. She focused on the silver mistwolf, seeing through Storm's golden eyes, feeling warm, silver fur covering her body, strong muscles running on lanky legs—

"Storm."

Adriane moved silently across the glade, her jewel pulsing in steady rhythm with her heart. Closing her eyes, she steadied herself. She needed to do this, she *had* to do this, or everything she loved would be lost. Storm needed help, Dreamer had been taken away, and the forest sylph was in trouble. It was all connected, she was sure of it.

The gentle pull of something familiar touched her mind. Adriane grabbed for it, focusing her will through her gem. With a flash, the trees suddenly seemed to come alive, glowing silvery green around the edges.

Adriane pushed harder, grasping for the part of her that was wolf, losing herself in the need to find her pack mate.

She could almost hear the echoing refrains of the lost mistwolves.

She staggered forward as her jewel started shifting

through colors. Was she making all this happen? Fire sprang forth, swirling up her arm and surrounding her in a halo of flickering light.

Throwing back her head, she howled.

An answering growl sliced through the air, getting closer. Adriane could smell the animal. It was hunting her.

Adriane tried to focus on Ravenswood, on Storm, but she was trapped inside a spinning kaleidoscope. Fear tore through her like an electric shock. Without Dreamer to help her or Storm to guide her, she was completely lost in the twisting and shifting magic.

"Storm!" she called out with all her strength.

The world spun as the wolf stone exploded in a jarring blaze of light.

She was in the magic glade—inches away from an enormous, gleaming spiderweb. Oily, silver strands hung from the trees. Adriane's heart raced with fear.

She tried to steady herself and calm her sparking gem. "Orenda, where are you?"

The spiderweb throbbed and twisted. Suspended in its center, a cocoon pulsed. The fairy creature trapped inside screamed, her pure magic consumed by the suffocating strands.

"Orenda!" Adriane staggered as she tried to use her magic to help the dying sylph. Time seemed to slow down as the warrior fought to stay on her feet. Her wolf stone was glowing a fierce, deep red. She reached deep inside herself, trying to find her own magic, but it was trapped, just as Orenda was locked in the shimmering prison.

Suddenly a blur of light shot from the shadows. She whirled and saw the glowing outline of the ghost wolf, lips pulled back in a death grin. Blue light exploded, stinging her like burning-hot embers. Warped red light shot from the wolf stone as Adriane rolled, trying to get to her feet. But the ghost wolf was standing over her, lips pulled back in a deadly grin.

"You should not hunt alone," he sneered.

Adriane stared into his shining animal eyes. "Who are you?"

"I am the pack leader." He lunged, jaws opened wide. *"Your wolf belongs to me!"*

Out of nowhere, a silver shape smashed the ghost wolf broadside, knocking him away.

Adriane rolled to her feet, jewel pulsing. "Stormbringer!"

Storm locked her golden eyes onto Adriane. *"You must leave!"*

The two wolves rammed together in battle, ripping and tearing at each other's haunches.

"No!" Adriane cried.

Fierce roars tore across the glade, but she was already being pulled downward. Bright colors flashed past her in swirling arcs as she fell from the spirit world.

She landed hard, jewel pulsing with her fear. Rolling over, she found herself nose to nose with Ozzie.

"Wow!" Ozzie yelled, fuzzy ferret hair standing on end. "What a rush!"

❧   ❧   ❧

Adriane pulled the blanket around her shoulders and clutched the steaming cup of cocoa on the kitchen table. She was completely exhausted—physically, magically, and emotionally. She looked into her mug, uncomfortably aware of Emily, Kara, Ozzie, Ariel, and Lyra all staring at her.

"We told you not to go off on your own!" Kara burst out.

"What if something had happened to you?" Emily added angrily.

Adriane sat quietly, head lowered.

"If Ozzie, Lyra, and Ariel hadn't followed you, we don't know what would have happened!" Kara continued.

"One minute you're in the glade, and the next you just disappeared." Ozzie waved his paws in the air.

"I didn't mean to scare you," Adriane said, rubbing her wolf stone. It was gold again—for now.

"What happened?" Emily asked.

"My jewel started going nuts, and then she just fell out of thin air!" Ozzie exclaimed, leaping up and down.

"Calm down, Ozzie," Emily said. "She's okay."

"She must have locked onto Ozzie's jewel to send me back," Adriane mused.

"Who?" Emily asked.

"Stormbringer."

"Wait," Emily gasped. "You saw Stormbringer?"

"Are you sure you weren't dreaming?" Kara asked.

"No." Adriane looked quickly at her friends. "I've seen her before."

Kara and Emily exchanged a glance.

"Storm helped me heal Dreamer in New Mexico. She sent me the magic of the spirit pack."

"And this time?" Emily asked gently.

"This time I think I actually moved between the real world and the spirit world," Adriane said. "She saved me from the other ghost wolf."

"I knew you were going to try that world walking stuff," Ozzie said, straightening his collar.

Adriane sat forward. "I think that wolf attacked Gran."

Emily pushed away from the table and stood up. "But if this wolf is in the spirit world, how could it attack Gran?"

"Through Dreamer."

"I still can't even reach the d'flies," Kara sighed. "We're cut off from the Fairy Realms and Aldenmor."

"This is all about me," Adriane said quietly.

"Not possible. It's always all about me," Kara quipped.

Emily elbowed the blazing star. "Adriane, anything that affects you affects all of us."

"I've lost Dreamer." Adriane looked at her friends, eyes wide with fear. "I'm going to lose my home, my family—everything."

"Someone's targeting you," Lyra growled.

"Hooo?" Ariel asked.

"Tell us what you saw," Emily said.

"The sylph was caught in a spiderweb. The glade was covered in them."

"I've seen those before," the blazing star said. "In the castle of the Spider Witch."

"But she's in the Otherworlds—" Ozzie broke off. "Uh-oh."

"And the Dark Sorceress is with her," Emily finished.

The mages and animals looked at one another, a stunned silence settling over the table.

"They're free," Adriane said, "and they're trying to destroy Ravenswood."

Chapter 7

"**H**ey Adriane, wait up!"

Outside the math classroom a lanky, dark-haired boy rushed to catch up with her. "This isn't really your last week of school, is it?" Joey asked, concerned.

"I don't know," Adriane said shyly as they walked out the front doors of the school. "I hope not."

"Me, too," he said with a hopeful smile.

Adriane started to return his smile, then froze. It seemed like half the student body of Stonehill Middle School had been waiting for her. They swarmed around her, abuzz with rumors.

"Everyone says your wolf attacked a bunch of old ladies!" Heather, a friend of Kara's, pushed to the front of the group, followed by Molly and Tiffany.

"That's not what happened," Adriane protested.

"The leopard ate Emily's ferret," Kyle, Kara's older brother, announced.

"Is it true Ravenswood is being shut down?" Marcus asked.

"I don't—" Adriane faltered, trying to make her way through the crowd. All she wanted to do was go home.

"Adriane, are you really leaving?" someone at the back of the group shouted.

"You can't leave!" Heather suddenly exclaimed.

"No way," Molly agreed.

"I mean . . ." Heather flushed. "We've put a lot of work into the preserve, too."

Adriane was stunned. Less than a year ago, these kids had made fun of her—now they were suddenly on her side?

"We heard the council is going to shut Ravenswood down!" a kid called out.

"We have to keep it open!" Molly declared.

"Save Ravenswood!" Joey shouted loudly.

A chant erupted from the crowd as kids cheered and clapped. "Save Ravenswood! Save Ravenswood!"

"No pictures, please," Kara's voice rang out as she pushed through the mob and slipped her arm through the warrior's. "How're you holding up?"

"A little overwhelmed," Adriane admitted.

"No one said being popular was easy." Kara smiled.

"Save the animals!" Emily called out, hurrying over as she stuffed her flute case in her backpack. "Wow, word spreads pretty fast around here."

"Come on, K., what's really going on at Ravenswood?" Tiffany asked Kara.

"Absolutely nothing is going on at Ravenswood," Kara declared. "Everything is perfectly fine."

"Help!"

The mages jumped as Ozzie's panicked voice blared in their minds.

"GAH!"

"Ozzie, what's wrong?" Emily responded to the frantic ferret telepathically.

"The portal is opening!" Ozzie screamed.

❂   ❂   ❂

Wind whipped the trees as Adriane raced from the woods into the field, Emily and Kara close behind. A swirling circle hung in the sky. Veiled by a rippling curtain of mist, a giant dreamcatcher flashed inside.

"Keep your wings, paws, and hooves away from the portal!" Ozzie commanded as Lyra herded brimbees, quiffles, and jeeran back from the immense doorway in the sky.

Adriane's wolf stone throbbed with pulsing light as the dreamcatcher stretched and warped.

"Something's trying to break through the dreamcatcher!" Ozzie exclaimed, smoothing his static-charged hair as the mages surrounded him.

Adriane stared at the glowing portal nervously. The dreamcatcher was designed to keep out anything that might hurt Ravenswood. "Everyone, take position!" she ordered.

Emily and Kara stood on either side of the warrior, flanked by Ozzie and Lyra.

Head pounding, Adriane jumped as her wolf stone suddenly flashed. She cracked it like a whip, sending golden sparks flying.

Get a grip, she told herself.

"Try to strengthen the dreamcatcher!" Emily called, sensing the warrior's uncertainty.

Girls and ferret aimed their gleaming jewels. Shimmering streaks of gold, white, blue, amber, red, and pink sizzled over the glowing portal, lighting the sky like fireworks. The curtain ripped open wider, revealing more of the finely woven web.

"That's not the dreamcatcher," Kara said grimly.

"Then what is it?" Emily asked.

"Ewww, it's a spiderweb!" a baby quiffle squealed.

The ground shook as something slammed into the web. A wave of power crashed over Adriane.

"What should we do?" Rasha shouted.

All eyes turned to Adriane.

Fear washed through her. Her friends were counting on her. But how was she supposed to be a warrior without her pack mate?

A terrifying howl echoed from the portal.

"Stay cool," Kara ordered the group of frightened animals. "Whatever it is, we can handle it!"

The howls grew into a wailing chorus, sending tendrils of web whipping loose like torn flags. The spiderweb was unraveling.

Adriane flashed on the savage apparition that had attacked her. This was a pack of them, their collective will bent on reaching Ravenswood. She struggled to focus as raw power surged through the wolf stone. Blinding colors swirled, stabbing her eyes and piercing her mind.

Suddenly the wolf stone erupted.

"Ahhh!" Animals dove as magic fire flew everywhere.

"I can't control it!" Adriane screamed, frantically trying to keep her fire away from the terrified animals.

"Emily!" Kara swung her sparkling red, white, and pink magic toward the warrior. "Help her!"

Adriane felt tingling, cool magic wrap the wolf stone in healing power. She tried to connect with her friends, but all she could feel was the creatures' need to break through. Emily and Kara were using all their magic to help her instead of trying to close the portal. She was going to fail when she was most needed.

Instinctively, Adriane reached for the presence that always kept her strong. But Dreamer wasn't there.

Instead, she felt the touch of another magic, offering her the support she so desperately needed. The powerful presence enveloped her, protected her, filling her with pure and unconditional love. Adriane grasped for it like a lifeline.

The warrior smiled, never wanting to let go of the comforting magic. "Thank you," she whispered.

"It's opening!" Ozzie's scream pierced the swirling winds.

With a final fiery explosion, the glowing spiderweb disintegrated, ripping the portal open in a flash of brilliant red.

Adriane staggered back as mistwolves, teeth bared and snarling, leaped over the mages, landing among the terrified animals.

"Incom-*agk!*" Ozzie yelped.

Something huge and red plummeted from the portal and landed with a booming thud. This creature was definitely not a mistwolf.

"Mama!"

Adriane blinked. An enormous red dragon the size of a school bus sat in the middle of the field—with a grinning blond-haired boy astride his back.

"Drake!" She stumbled over to the creature and hugged his broad neck.

"Mama!" the dragon shouted, wagging his spiked tail, scattering mistwolves and animals everywhere. He dropped his enormous head, hiding the girl under a puff of steam.

"Thought you could use a friend." The boy slid off the dragon, slipping his flying gloves in his wide black belt.

"Zach!" Her two best friends from Aldenmor had come for her.

"You did say to drop by any—" Zach was cut off as Adriane caught him in a bear hug.

"I missed you, too." Zach returned her hug warmly.

Adriane stepped away shyly, wiping her cheeks. "And my baby boy," Adriane said, rubbing Drake between his eye ridges, making the dragon snort with pleasure. "It was you who grabbed on to me, wasn't it."

"Drake's magic can be pretty intense," Zach said, his bright red dragon stone shining from a brown leather band on his wrist. "He doesn't know his own strength."

"Wolf sister." A huge mistwolf approached, fur black as night and golden eyes gleaming.

"Moonshadow." Adriane knelt and hugged the pack leader, nose to nose.

"I have brought twenty-four of the pack to help protect the forest."

The mistwolf pack gathered around the mages, welcoming them with a frenzy of wagging tails, grinning faces, and low howls of excitement. The sun gleamed off their lustrous coats of silver, auburn, brown, blue, and diamond white. They were magnificent.

"This is incredible!" Emily breathed.

Adriane felt exhilarated as the magic of the pack filled her. She was being welcomed as an equal. A beautiful gold-and-white wolf nosed her way past Moonshadow.

"We are sorry for the pain caused by our arrival. There was no other way."

"We'll live," Adriane smiled.

"This is Dawnrunner," Moonshadow growled. "My mate."

"You honor me." The warrior bowed to the magnificent she-wolf.

The wolves lifted their heads and howled as one. The wolfsong rang over the field.

"Get off me, you big lizard!" Ozzie pushed his way out from under Drake's belly, smoothing his singed and ruffled fur.

Drake pressed a giant golden eye close to the ferret's head. "Hi!"

"A Knight of the Circle is a friend to the mistwolves," Dawnrunner said.

"Gah!"

"Welcome to Ravenswood." The blazing star smiled at the new arrivals. "And are we glad to see you!"

"Hello." Drake bent his head around Kara and peered down at the curious animals.

"Hey, watch it!" Kara covered her hair. "I just had it highlighted!"

"Drake's perfectly friendly," Zach reassured the quivering quiffles.

"We will check the forests." Dawnrunner nudged the pack leader's side as she led the other wolves into the trees. In an instant they vanished, as if swallowed by the woods.

Moonshadow growled. "She is concerned."

"What's happening to Ravenswood?" Emily asked.

"There is a field of dark magic covering this entire forest," Zach explained. "Drake was the only one strong enough to break through."

"No wonder the d'flies couldn't hear me," Kara exclaimed.

"I broke the portal!" Drake announced proudly.

"Good boy." Adriane kissed his big red nose.

"Awww, he's portal trained." Kara smiled.

With a sudden spark, the roiling mesh of webbing magically wove back, sealing the portal shut. In a rush of wind, it vanished.

"We could be here a while," Zach observed.

"There's plenty of room for everyone," Emily stated.

"Where's Dreamer?" Zach asked, sudden concern in his eyes.

Adriane's smile faded. "He's been taken away."

Zach's dragon stone flashed in alarm.

"Something's wrong with his magic," Adriane said.

"It affects all mistwolves," Moonshadow snarled.

"You mean it's not just Dreamer?" Adriane asked. "What happened?"

"The spirit pack is missing," the wolf answered.

"Missing?" Orenda had told Adriane to find missing mistwolves.

"Our magic comes from the spirit pack," the pack leader explained. *"Without them, it will fade until it is lost forever."*

90

Adriane stared into the wolf's deep golden eyes, sensing how much had been sacrificed to come here. "That's why Dreamer couldn't turn to mist, why I couldn't talk to him."

"I have brought the strongest of the pack." The wolf lowered his head before Adriane. *"In this forest, we will make our stand."*

He was submitting to her leadership.

The warrior knelt and raised his head, looking at the pack leader eye to eye. "We must find the spirit pack."

"There's more," Zach said gravely. "The Dark Sorceress and the Spider Witch have escaped the Otherworlds. This dark magic is their work."

"Tell us something we don't know," Kara quipped.

"She's located another power crystal," Zach said.

"That'll do," Kara conceded.

"Why are they attacking Ravenswood?" Emily asked. "What's the connection?"

"We don't know yet. The Fairimentals tried to warn you, but they couldn't break through—" Zach looked around. "Where is the Experimental Fairimental, Tweek?"

"He exploded two days ago, and we haven't seen him since," Ozzie grumbled.

"Let's go back to my house and we'll tell you all about it," Adriane said.

As Emily and Kara started walking across the

field, Adriane was practically giddy with relief. The situation was bad, but the pack, Drake, and Zach filled her with strength and new hope.

"I see you've been getting the Fred-X deliveries," Adriane said, observing Zach's outfit of black Gap jeans, tan sweater, and down vest.

"Thanks for all the care packages." Zach smiled, pushing his neatly trimmed blond hair away from his eyes. "I'm the best-dressed boy on Aldenmor."

"You're the only boy on Aldenmor," Kara remarked.

Adriane noticed Zach had filled out. The soft features of his face now angled into a strong chin that set off his sparkling blue eyes. Broad shoulders and strong arms framed his tall physique.

"Drake looks good," she observed. "You have really taken care of each other."

He smiled. "You look good, too, Adriane."

Adriane felt heat flare over her cheeks.

"What else did the Fairimentals say?" Emily asked Zach.

"The spirit of Ravenswood is being twisted by strong elemental magic."

"That would be one Spider Witch, thank you very much," Kara said.

"The forest sylph is under attack." Adriane scanned the thick trees, sensing the dark force worming its way through the forest.

"These are magical woods." Moonshadow sniffed the air. *"It is no wonder the spirit trail runs through here."*

Adriane turned to the pack leader. Is that what she had experienced? The spirit trail?

"When the spirit pack vanished, we lost the spirit trail. No one can find it. Soon our magic will fade completely."

"Moonshadow," Adriane said, passing under the huge oaks bordering the trail to her house. "I have seen the spirit pack."

The wolf stared at Adriane. *"You saw ten thousand mistwolves?"*

"No. One."

"How?" Zach asked, genuinely impressed.

"I don't really know," she admitted. "Tweek called it world walking."

"You are bonded to the mistwolves," Moonshadow said, as if that explained everything. *"What did this mistwolf look like?"*

"He was silver and black," Adriane said, shivering with the memory of the fierce creature. "With one blue eye and one green eye. He called himself the pack leader."

"Chain!" Moonshadow barked.

"Who's that?" Emily asked.

"Chain was pack leader before me," Moonshadow said. *"When he died, he refused to join the spirit pack with the rest of our ancestors. Instead, he turned rogue."*

"But why?" Adriane asked.

A low growl rumbled from the black wolf. *"He was betrayed by his human bonded and left in dishonor."*

"Betrayed?" Adriane was stunned.

"Who was his bonded?" Zach asked.

"A human wizard called Gardener."

The mages gasped.

"I don't believe it!" Kara said.

"I forbade the mistwolves contact with humans because I thought they would all betray us." The powerful black wolf turned his deep golden eyes on Adriane. *"I was wrong."*

But evidently one did, Adriane thought. How could that be possible? The records they had found in Gardener's secret room seemed to indicate he was totally dedicated to saving the wolves.

"Chain is a vengeful spirit," Moonshadow continued. *"And very dangerous."*

"But I have seen another," Adriane said. "Stormbringer."

The wolf's golden eyes were wide with amazement. *"I knew I was right to come here."*

Storm had died to save the mistwolves, but now the pack was in terrible danger again. They were counting on Adriane. She hadn't even been able to save Dreamer—how could she save the entire mistwolf pack?

"This is where I live," Adriane said to Zach and Moonshadow as they left the trees and headed over the grass behind the cottage.

"Really cool." The boy smiled, taking in the wood and red brick house nestled peacefully in the forest. In the distance, Ravenswood Manor loomed, its Gothic towers dark and imposing.

"What do we do with the big guy?" Kara said, pointing to Drake. The dragon was curiously examining the stone chimney.

"Ozzie, you'll be in charge of our guests," Emily said.

"Great . . ."

Several mistwolves appeared from the bushes, sniffing out the grounds.

"Do *not* eat the quiffles!" the ferret shouted.

"I think I know what's going on," Kara said suddenly.

"What?" Emily asked.

"We've seen this happen before. It could only be—"

"My mom!" Adriane exclaimed.

"Gag! How could she be responsible?" Ozzie asked, wiping dragon slobber off his head.

The warrior urgently tried to push Drake into the shrubbery. "You have to hide!"

"Adriane?"

The warrior turned to see her mother rounding the path from the main driveway. Willow stopped dead in her tracks, dark eyes open wide in surprise.

Chapter 8

Adriane whirled around, her heart hammering. Emily, Kara, Zach, and Ariel waved at her. Drake and the mistwolves were nowhere in sight. Only a faint mist floated through the trees.

"I could have sworn I saw—" Willow began, then shook her head. "Must have been the sun in my eyes."

"Hi, I'm Kara. This is Emily and Zach," the blazing star said as the sounds of cracking and crunching faded behind them.

"I'm sorry we were not properly introduced," Willow said, and smiled. "I'm Willow Charday."

Emily stepped forward, red curls bouncing. Ariel sat on her shoulder, blinking great big owl eyes. "It's very nice to meet you, Mrs.—"

"Please call me Willow."

"This is Ariel," Emily said. "She lives here with Adriane."

"Hoolow."

"She's beautiful." Then Willow eyed the blond boy warily. "Do you live around here, Zach?"

"I uh, live over on Alden—"

"Allentown," Kara finished quickly. "Part of an interschool program to help the preserve."

"That's quite a ways to come to work here," Willow noted.

"This is a special place." He smiled, glancing at Adriane. "I'd like to visit more often."

Adriane turned beet red. Then her mother's voice brought her back to Earth.

"—supposed to meet us at the hotel right after school," she said.

Adriane frowned. "Um, I had chores and I needed help taking care of things around here."

"Maybe you're taking on more than you can handle," Willow said.

You have no idea, Adriane thought.

"Adriane told us you were in Philadelphia exhibiting Mr. Charday's new sculptures," Emily said cheerily.

"Actually, they're not sculptures," Kara explained. "They're free-form light modules."

"You know your art, Kara." Willow was impressed.

"My mom is on the board of the Hammersmith," Kara beamed. "She showed me the program last night."

Emily and Adriane looked at her in amazement.

"What? It's an art gallery," Kara told them.

"Adriane," Willow said softly. "Can we talk . . . inside?"

Adriane turned and stomped up the porch to the front door. She glanced at Zach, and her jewel flashed. *"Keep Drake away while I talk to my mom."*

"We have to finish up those chores now," Emily said, running into the woods.

"Right. It was nice to see you again." Kara waved as she and Zach raced after the healer.

"Your friends are certainly active."

"You should see them on a good day," Adriane said.

They entered the foyer and Willow stopped, taking in the cozy living room. Flowery drapes fluttered in the gentle breeze, slanting soft light over the family pictures on the mantel.

Willow gazed at the photos, her eyes resting on her wedding portrait. "Seems like only yesterday that I left this place."

Adriane followed her mother into the kitchen.

"I brought you something." Willow carefully took a book out of her bag and handed it to Adriane. "This edition has some really cool artwork."

Adriane ran her fingers over the rich leather and gold embossed title: *Alice in Wonderland*. Her favorite. When she was younger, Adriane had always dreamed of being like Alice and finding her own special wonderland. "Thank you."

Willow opened a cabinet and smiled. "Peppermint tea. Gran always kept it here."

She filled a pot with water and set it on the burner.

"When I first met your father, I knew I wanted to be with him more than anything." Willow smiled wistfully. "You should see his new pieces, Adriane. They're his best ever."

"I'm sure they are."

"You know, he talks about you all the time." Willow started to pull out Gran's usual chair at the table, then paused and sat in the chair next to it. "Adriane, why didn't you call us after Gran's accident?"

The warrior placed the book on the counter. What did her mom expect her to say? Because you'd show up and ruin everything for me. And, by the way, thanks for letting them take Dreamer!

"Have you wondered how we got here so fast?" Willow asked suddenly, fidgeting with the silver rings shining on her slim fingers.

Adriane blinked, surprised. "Didn't the hospital call you?"

Willow locked her dark eyes on Adriane. "Gran told me."

"B-but—" Adriane stammered.

"In a dream. Does that sound strange?"

This was the first time her mom had talked about anything like this.

Willow gestured to Adriane's chair. "Please, Adriane. Sit with me."

The warrior hesitated, then slowly walked over and sat down.

"The truth is, I never felt comfortable at Ravenswood. "

Adriane looked down at her hands, her voice strained. "Then how come you left me here?"

"Gran insisted you be here when you became a teenager. That woman is pure stubborn."

"I'm glad she did."

"You've changed, Adriane. I can see it, so beautiful and strong." Willow's slender fingers brushed the hair from Adriane's face. "You've blossomed here."

Adriane shuffled in her chair but didn't move away.

Willow leaned forward. "But we have to deal with reality. Gran is very sick."

"She'll get better," Adriane vowed. Please, she prayed with all her might, she has to.

"I think you've inherited more than her stubborn streak," Willow said with a fleeting smile. "You're more like her than I ever was."

"You say that like it's a bad thing."

"She is very . . . passionate about Ravenswood." Willow got up and brought the teapot to the table. She poured steaming tea in their cups. "When I was your age, all she talked about was our heritage and how it's linked to nature. She said we could talk to forest spirits. I get scared watching *Casper*." She smiled, waiting for Adriane to say something. "I can see this is making you upset. I'm sorry."

Adriane struggled with her thoughts, trying to explain what she was going through, what was really happening. Instead, she went back to what was familiar: her anger. "I'm upset because you're ruining my life!"

"What do you propose I do, Adriane?" Willow's voice raised in frustration. "You're thirteen years old. You can't live here alone."

"Ravenswood is my home. It's the only one I've ever really had, thanks to you."

Adriane stood and walked to the sink, hair falling over her face.

"That wolf. Is that what we're talking about? You can get lots of pets—"

"Dreamer!" Adriane swung around. "His name is Dreamer, Mother!"

"A wild wolf, Adriane. That's not normal," Willow insisted.

Adriane paced defiantly. "Different cities for a few months, then onto somewhere new. You call that normal?" She fought back tears. "I never knew where we'd be going next. How was I supposed to make friends when I'd be gone in six months?"

"You don't understand," Willow pleaded.

"No. I get it. *You* were never happy here, and now you don't want me to be happy."

"Of course I do, honey. I'm glad you've made friends here. But we need to be a family—"

"We needed to be a family ten years ago." Her anger spent, Adriane slumped back into the chair.

The two Charday women sat quietly, the ticktock of the kitchen wall clock filling in the silence.

"Adriane," Willow finally spoke. "Your father has been offered a grant at the Reisfeld Foundation. It's a very prestigious gallery in Woodstock, New York."

Adriane sat up. "New York?"

"We plan to buy a house and settle there. You could work with your father on your art. And we could visit Manhattan together—wouldn't that be exciting?"

"I don't want to live there!"

Suddenly a huge golden dragon eye covered the kitchen window.

"Mama?" Drake's voice rumbled in her head.

"Drake, I'm okay!" Adriane's jewel sparked as she tried to calm the dragon.

The dragon eye slowly inched out of sight as Ozzie, Emily, Kara, Lyra, Ariel, and Zach dragged him off by the tail.

"Adriane?" Willow was staring at the wolf stone. "Where did you get that jewel?"

"I, uh . . ." Awkwardly, she covered her bracelet. "It was a gift."

Willow sighed. "You've made some kind of connection to this place, Adriane, and frankly, it scares me to death."

"I . . ." How much did her mother really know about Ravenswood? How could she talk about something that wasn't supposed to be real? "What will happen to the preserve if I leave?"

"That's up to the town council."

"I have to stay here!" Adriane pleaded.

"Why?"

"To find out . . ."

"Find out what, Adriane?"

"Who I am."

A huge dragon eyeball popped in front of the window again, followed by a quick turn of his head, a roar, and a blazing burst of fire.

"What is going on out there?" Willow jumped up and opened the back door.

"Ahhhhh!" Ozzie flew by, tail smoking.

Kara, Emily, and Zach skidded around the corner and barged inside.

"Is everything okay?" Willow asked.

"Couldn't be better—why?" Kara smiled.

Willow turned to her daughter. "Your father and I leave for New York on Saturday. You need to be packed and ready," she said quietly, giving Adriane a quick hug.

"Ow." Ozzie walked inside, rubbing his rear end.

Willow glanced at him quickly, then shook her

head and walked to the front door. "It was nice to see all of you."

The warrior watched her mother close the door.

Adriane stomped to the living room and sat on the couch. "What am I going to do? They're going to make me leave and then turn the preserve over to the council."

"You can't leave!" Kara exclaimed.

"We have to do something!" Ozzie declared.

"And we don't have much time," Emily added.

Adriane glanced at Kara. "Any more bright ideas, Miss Artypants?"

"As a matter of fact, Morticia, yes." Kara signaled to the mistwolves, brimbees, and quiffles that were all pressing their noses to the cottage's windows. "Group huddle!"

The animals piled inside, cramming through the back door and shuffling through the kitchen. Once again, Adriane's house was packed with animals.

"Everyone here?" Kara called out.

A loud *thud* sounded at the front door.

"Who is that?" Emily whispered.

"I thought she left." Adriane nervously opened the door a crack—revealing a big red dragon snout.

"*I help?*" Drake asked, peering inside at the overcrowded living room.

"Of course." She hugged the dragon so hard he started purring like a buzzsaw. "Why don't you just stay right there," she said, bringing a few pillows from the couch to prop up his head.

Drake squeezed his massive head through the front door, settling just outside the living room.

Zach turned to Adriane. "Everyone filled me in while you were talking with your mom."

"We need a plan, but we still don't know exactly what we're up against," Adriane said.

"Maybe we do," Kara mused, looking at the group. "I think a power crystal landed in the astral planes."

"Is that even possible?" Emily asked.

"A crystal ended up in the Otherworlds," Kara pointed out. "It turned the Fairy Realms upside down. It's doing the same thing to the astral planes."

"So why is the witch attacking the Ravenswood sylph?" Adriane asked. "What's the connection?"

"She can't find the crystal," Zach exclaimed. "She's using the forest spirit to attract it."

"Magic attracts magic," Ozzie reminded them.

"And only a mistwolf could bring the crystal from the spirit world to the real world," Moonshadow growled.

"Dreamer is a gifted magic tracker," Adriane said.

"Gifted enough to walk the spirit world without the spirit trail," Dawnrunner said.

"But why Adriane?" Emily asked. "We're all tied to the magic of Ravenswood."

Adriane raised her amber wolf stone.

"They get to you, they get Dreamer," Zach concluded.

"And now he's all alone!" Adriane began pacing.

Kara had her cell in her hand, beeping up a storm.

"Gran got sick because of all this," Adriane realized, anger and fear surging through her. "I'm responsible. Ravenswood is going be destroyed because of me."

"We won't let that happen," Zach said determinedly, dragon stone gleaming.

Moonshadow rose. *The mistwolves stand with Ravenswood!"*

Adriane knew what she had to do.

"He's being held at the Amazing Adventure Animal Park," Kara said, clicking off her phone.

"That's almost three hours away!" Emily exclaimed.

Adriane walked over and kissed the Drake's nose. "I'd say more like twenty minutes."

Then she turned and bowed to Moonshadow and Dawnrunner. "I am a warrior, sister of the mistwolves." The wolf stone reflected the determination in her dark eyes. "And I am going to save my pack mate!"

Chapter 9

His magnificent wings angled back, Drake dove through light cloud cover, soaring over the sprawling animal park. The three mages huddled behind Zach on the dragon's back.

Adriane sat behind Zach, Kara in the rear. In the middle, Emily gazed over the gingko and baobab trees dotting the plains below. "We're over the African Savannah."

"Safari so good. Lyra, what can you see?" Kara called out.

Golden wings shimmering against the night, Lyra dropped from the clouds and came up alongside the dragon. Ozzie rode on her back. *"The guards are approaching the yak corral."*

"Good." Kara squashed the map she had printed from the park's Web site, trying to keep it from blowing away. "There's a jungle garden behind the aviary. Over that way."

With a touch from Zach, the dragon responded instantly, banking left and gliding low over a panicked herd of zebra.

"Doesn't seem natural to have so many animals penned up," the boy observed.

"It's for their own good," Emily responded, sounding surprisingly like her mother. "They're taken care of here, and zoologists do research to learn more about them and how to save them in the wild."

"It's so different here."

"Wait till you see the mall," Kara said excitedly.

Adriane watched the boy and dragon fly together, perfectly in sync. She recognized the low-slung leather saddle and attached saddlebags: They once belonged to a griffin named Winddancer, Zach's former bonded magical animal. Windy had sacrificed himself to save Zach and Adriane. Despite his grief, Zach had opened his heart to Drake. The bond between them now was strong and confident.

Adriane turned her attention to the animal park and tried to focus on connecting with her own bonded, Dreamer. But all she got was the buzzing of hundreds of different wildlife.

"Six o'clock." Kara pointed to a large building spiked with a wire-mesh roof. It was next to the main zoo, where animals lived in wide, spacious pens.

"Take us in, Drake." Zach's dragon stone pulsed bright red as he guided the dragon over a dark canopy of green trees. "Hold on!"

"Wha-aaaaaaaaht?"

Drake dropped, his huge feet cushioning the

landing as they crunched to a jarring stop. They were in the middle of a dense tropical jungle.

"He said hold on," Adriane called over Emily's shoulder as she swung off the dragon.

"Next time, speak up." The blazing star landed daintily on her pink sneakers, trying to gauge just how muddy this rescue mission could get.

The garden enveloped them in the scent of sweet flowers mingled with the soft mist of the mini rain forest. Chirping birds filled the air as the larger predators in the aviary squawked out warnings.

"Next time, call a taxi," the windblown ferret said through chattering teeth. He slid from Lyra's back as the cat landed gracefully.

The group peered from the garden onto the pathway that circled the aviary. On the far side it forked— one path toward Polar Bear Cove, the other to the Elephant Camp.

Kara smoothed the map, illuminating it with a pinpoint of light from her unicorn jewel. "There are administration buildings—here, here, and here."

Emily peered over Kara's shoulder. "Does it say where the hospital or lab is? That would be where they keep new animals."

Adriane turned away from her friends and held up her jewel, sending golden rays into the night like a beacon.

"Turn that off!" Kara cried, pulling the warrior's arm down. "Someone's going to see that!"

The warrior angrily shook off Kara. "I don't need a map to find Dreamer."

"The key word is 'find him without getting our rear ends caught.' "

"That's eight words," Ozzie corrected.

Zach led Drake back into the colorful flora. "Drake, you stay here and hide while we look around, okay?"

Drake snorted, settling his bulk gingerly in a patch of ferns, tail flattening a dozen bushes.

"Lyra, up and at 'em," Kara ordered. "You see anything with two legs, give me a shout."

"Right." The cat spread her wings and took off, disappearing into the night sky.

"Let's head to the conservation center," Kara said, heading to the left.

Adriane started walking in the opposite direction.

Ozzie looked from the blazing star to the warrior.

"I'll go with Adriane." Zach shrugged, walking off behind the warrior. "Emily and Ozzie, go with Kara."

"Fine!" Kara called out. "We'll cover more ground if we split up, anyway."

The warrior hurried away, dark eyes flashing. Time was slipping away. She shook her jewel and tried to sense Dreamer, pull him to her. Red heat flared over her wrist, and she gasped.

Zach fell into step beside her. "What's wrong?"

"He's in trouble." Adriane spun to face the boy, fighting to control her emotions. "I can feel it."

"We'll find him." Zach looked at her, blue eyes full of understanding.

Adriane fell silent as they walked quickly past a pile of curious lemurs. Her heart pounded, tears welling in her eyes. "In my dreams, I try to save Storm, try to do things differently. But I wake up, and she's always gone."

"When Windy died, I kept telling myself there was something I could have done," Zach said quietly. "If only I'd known a little more magic, or if I'd been able to fly better . . ."

"You've done such an amazing job with Drake," Adriane said.

"Drake and I share something even more magical than a jewel."

"What's that?"

"You."

Adriane blushed. "Then I'm surprised you can still fly."

"Dreamer is special—even Moonshadow says so," Zach said. "And that wolf would rather eat his foot than say something complimentary."

"I couldn't help Dreamer, either, could I?" Adriane said quietly.

Zach stopped and took her hand in his. He focused on his dragon stone, adding his magic to hers.

The wolf stone suddenly flashed. Adriane's eyes went wide as she caught the sounds of ragged breathing, the cold glint of a steel cage.

"I felt something." Adriane swung her wrist up, trying to hone in on the magic. She sped ahead—and ran smack into Kara.

"Oof!" Kara bounced back into Emily, her unicorn jewel flashing with pinks and reds. "Well?"

Adriane shook her head, jewel fire dying. "I lost him."

"He's here somewhere," Kara stated, polishing her jewel with the sleeve of her black cashmere sweater.

Adriane glared at the blond girl. "I almost found him until you got in the way!"

"Where's Zach?" Ozzie asked, looking around in the dark.

"Great. You lost him, too," Kara said.

"Over here." Zach stood outside of the elephant pen. "These are remarkably intelligent animals."

"Africans," Emily said, walking to the pen. "You can tell from their ears." She pointed to the large, droopy ears fluttering like drapes.

"*Heads up.*" Lyra's voice suddenly popped in their minds. "*Two guards heading your way.*"

"What do we do?" Ozzie shuffled back and forth.

"Why not just ask *them*?" Kara asked sarcastically, pointing to the elephants.

"Good idea," Emily answered. "Ozzie?"

Ozzie straightened his ferret stone importantly. "Well, I have learned some interesting bytes from Tweek on interspecies communication."

Ferret stone flashing orange, Ozzie hopped up on the wall that separated the park visitors from the pen. "Hey, you!"

The largest elephant turned slowly, dropping a trunk full of hay. Its trunk snaked over and poked Ozzie in the stomach.

"Gah!"

"Try to make contact," Emily directed.

"I just did!" The ferret took a deep breath and concentrated. Soon his stone glowed bright gold as orange magic shimmered around the elephant.

Ozzie held up a paw and waved. "We come in peace!"

Water blasted from the elephant's trunk, dousing the ferret.

"FrruFpm!"

"Send the elephant a visual," Kara suggested.

Ozzie squeezed his eyes shut. His fur stood straight out as his ferret stone blasted a beam at the elephant.

Emily added a touch of her magic to Ozzie's as she faced the 10,000-pound pachyderm. "We're looking for a wolf who was brought here yesterday. Can you help us find our friend?"

The elephant waved his trunk, trumpeting to an

ostrich flock next door. An ostrich ran and stuck his head through the next fence over, screeching loudly to a sleeping zebra.

"They're talking to each other!" the healer exclaimed.

The zebra brayed at the Monkey House. A monkey leaped into a tree, gibbering and pointing excitedly across the path toward the reptile house.

"Oh, no," Ozzie said. "I am *not* talking to a snake!"

"There's a facility behind it," Emily said.

"Hurry, the guards are coming!" Lyra shouted, swooping by on her patrol.

"Let's go." Adriane sprinted past the wide Reptile Hut toward a secluded two-story adobe building.

She stopped at the bolted front door. A sign read, Authorized Personnel Only.

"We can't break in there!" Ozzie cried, stomping up behind her.

The warrior whipped golden fire into the air. With a loud *crack,* the magic blasted the door open.

"Well, maybe."

Alarms screeched through the night as floodlights blazed to life, illuminating the mages in fluorescent light.

"Very stealthy, Godzilla," Kara said, looking around nervously as her jewel light bounced off the dark interior.

"What was that?" Lyra cried.

"We're rescuing," Kara called back.

"Can you do it a little more quietly?"

"This way!" Adriane rushed down the dimly lit corridor, Zach and the others close behind. Growling and hooting echoed through the hallway as the animals inside reacted to the piercing alarms.

Adriane scanned every room, her wolf light ricocheting off the metal walls. "There!" She ran to the end of the corridor, smashing the door open.

The large room was full of instruments and tables. A row of steel cages lined the far wall, filled with parrots, a puma, and a baby monkey. Adriane's heart leaped to her throat as she saw the sheen of black fur in the corner cage.

"Dreamer!" the warrior cried, running to her pack mate.

The wolf lunged, slamming into the bars.

"Adriane!" Zach grabbed the warrior's arm.

She shook off Zach's hand and reached to open the cage.

"Adriane, wait!" Emily shouted, healing gem blazing with blue light.

"We have to get him out!" Adriane screamed as Dreamer crashed into the bars again.

Blazing heat seared into Adriane's mind. Pinpoints of red spread before her eyes. She spun away from her friends. With a blast of fire, the cage burst open.

The mistwolf slammed into her chest, snapping viciously at her throat.

"Dreamer!" Adriane fell backward into an examination table, sending instruments flying. Golden fire exploded from her wrist, wrapping her in a coil of protective magic as she tried to fend off the attack. The room lit up in jewel fire as the mages sent blue, red, pink, and orange magic streaming into the wolf.

The world wavered and drifted away as Adriane hit the cold cement floor. From the corner of her eye she saw the wolf's eyes flash red, a ghostly silver outline shimmering against his jet-black fur.

Zach was on Dreamer's back, trying to tear the thrashing wolf away from the mages.

"That's not Dreamer . . . ," Adriane whispered, not knowing whether anyone had heard her—

A familiar mocking voice echoed in her mind: *"How does it feel to betray your pack mate?"*

And she found herself standing in a vast field. A purple sky arced over feathery grass and flowers of red, blue, and green dancing in the wind.

Chain stood in the field, eyes focused on her with a malicious glare.

Wolf stone sparking, Adriane tried desperately to connect with her pack mate. She sensed Dreamer somewhere, submerged under Chain's control. But as her magic touched the ghostly outline, raw savagery overwhelmed her. Her lips drew back in a snarl.

"Let him go!" she yelled.

"Humans are all the same. Sooner or later, they will betray everything they love."

"I won't let you take him!"

"He's already gone." The wolf surged forward, then skidded to a stop.

Adriane raised her wolf stone, ready to strike. But it was not the wolf stone that reflected sudden fear in Chain's eyes. It was the silver wolf that stood at Adriane's side, ready to fight for her pack mate.

Breathing in deeply, Adriane wanted to laugh out loud as she filled with strength and confidence. She was whole again, as she hadn't been since—

Before Adriane could react, the two wolves hurled themselves forward head on, jaws open wide. With a vicious snarl, they crashed together. Teeth bared, Storm spun around and lunged for Chain's throat. Blue sparks ripped through the air as the two wolves collided in a blur of teeth and claws. Storm howled as Chain ripped at her haunches. Adriane watched in horror as Storm's ghostly outline shredded, mist trailing from her body.

"Storm!" Adriane staggered as a burst of swirling magic abruptly surrounded her, pulling her away.

"Drake, no!" the warrior screamed, unable to resist the dragon's powerful pull.

"Easy." Emily's face was full of concern as her healing gem bathed the warrior in cooling greens and blues.

The world came into focus.

Adriane was back in the lab. Everyone was yelling at once.

"Are you okay?"

"Can you walk?"

"Easy." Zach helped her to her feet, dragon stone flashing.

"What happened?" She held Zach's arm to steady herself until the room stopped spinning.

"You fell . . . and then you saved Dreamer."

Dreamer stood with his head lowered, tail between his legs, emerald eyes filled with shame.

Adriane grabbed the mistwolf in a fierce hug.

"He's okay, Adriane," Emily said. "You did it."

Sirens whined in the distance, fast approaching.

Kara ran to the window. "We've got company."

Harsh white lights cut through the windows as beams flew everywhere.

"We have to get out of here, *now!*" Ozzie shouted.

The building suddenly shook with a loud *thud* as something huge landed above them.

"Drake's on the roof," Zach said.

"Stairs!" Kara ordered.

The group barreled out the door and down the hall, scrambling up a flight of stairs. Bursting through the emergency exit, they piled onto the flat slate roof. In front of them the huge red dragon crouched low, wings spread, glinting eyes scanning the park. Beams of light swept over the creature as the sound of vehicles surrounded them.

Zach was in the saddle slipping on his flying gloves. He turned to help hoist Dreamer behind him as Adriane, Emily, and Kara climbed aboard.

Ozzie took a flying leap onto Lyra as she dove across the roof, gliding right off the opposite corner.

"Let's go!" Zach yelled.

Drake flapped his wings, sending a downdraft that rustled the trees as he flew high into the sky.

Adriane watched the building below shrink as guards ran inside armed with rifles and flashlights.

She tried to steady her breathing, holding tightly onto Dreamer. Then she realized Emily had been talking to her.

"You look as if you've seen a ghost." Emily bent down, healing stone flashing as she scanned the wolf.

Kara raised her arms in the air. "The team's back together again!"

Dreamer wagged his tail, licking all three mage faces at once.

"Wow, that was something!" Zach said.

"Bet life was pretty boring without us," Kara called out.

"No, but it was a lot less fun." Zach turned around, smiling. "You were great, Adriane—" He frowned when he saw Adriane's face. "What's wrong?"

"I didn't save Dreamer," she said. "Stormbringer did."

"How?" Emily asked.

"I don't know, but I saw her. She's fading fast."

"Which means time is running out for all the mist-wolves," Zach said grimly. "We've got to find the spirit pack."

"The pack must survive." Dreamer's eyes shone. *"We must run the spirit trail."*

Adriane bit her lip. Dreamer was right, but where would that path lead her? A deep emptiness dimmed the joy at rescuing her pack mate. For a few seconds, she and Storm had been connected, just like it used to be. The only thing Adriane could feel now was a terrible black hollowness clawing at her insides.

She hugged Dreamer, but her mind echoed with the words of Chain. *"You will betray your pack mate. Humans always do."*

Chapter 10

In the hunt, the wolf pack worked as a unit, many animals with one purpose. But this was no ordinary hunt. On this afternoon, the pack came together to hunt something not of this world.

Adriane ran her fingers through Dreamer's silky sun-warmed fur. "Are you ready?"

The mistwolf's emerald eyes flashed. *"I am always ready to run with you."*

"Moonshadow . . ."

The wolf looked at Adriane with piercing golden eyes.

"What happened to Chain?"

"He said he was left by his human to die." Moonshadow's rich voice echoed in her mind.

"But why? I don't understand how that could have happened."

"We thought Gardener was one of the good guys," Emily added.

"Not all humans are meant to run with us." The pack leader turned to Zach. *"I spent many years hating my wolf brother, blaming him for the death of our wolf mother."*

Adriane caught the flare of pain in Zach's eyes.

"*I was wrong. And I believe Chain is wrong as well.*" Moonshadow looked at Zach with a wolfish grin. "*And now I have my wolf brother back.*"

"*And his bonded,*" Dawnrunner added, lips drawn back in a smile.

Drake hopped from foot to foot, sending tremors across the glade.

Adriane studied the mistwolves who had risked everything for this hunt. The forests had strengthened their fading magic and they had strengthened Dreamer's, but it wouldn't last.

Moonshadow's powerful black body was highlighted by the towering Rocking Stone as he faced the pack.

"*We will send our wolf sister and pack mate to run the spirit trail, as mistwolves have done for thousands of years,*" the pack leader began.

Adriane nodded gratefully.

"*From our Circle of Protection, you will be rooted in this world,*" Dawnrunner explained.

"*But we cannot protect you if you wander from the path,*" Moonshadow warned, growling low.

Dawnrunner brushed against Adriane. The warrior knelt, nose to nose with the wolf. She felt hot breath on her neck as the wolf sniffed her, remembering her scent. "*If you lose your way, follow what is in your heart. That is the true path of a warrior.*"

"Thank you," Adriane said, and bowed her head. "We are ready."

The wolves fanned out, encircling Adriane. Emily, Kara, Lyra, Ozzie, Drake, and Zach joined them, leaving Adriane and Dreamer alone in the center.

Dreamer looked at his pack mate, love and determination shining in his emerald eyes. He would be by her side, keeping her safe.

Satisfied, Moonshadow addressed Adriane. *"You will have only a few minutes before we pull you back. Any longer is too dangerous."*

Adriane's pulse pounded. What if she couldn't find Storm? How was she going to hold on long enough to find the spirit pack *and* search for the power crystal?

"I don't know what I'm supposed to do," Adriane admitted.

"You are one of us," Dawnrunner told her. *"Listen."*

Adriane nodded. She *had* to succeed.

Dawnrunner began singing softly, a wandering tune that ebbed and flowed like the voice of the river. Adriane closed her eyes and drifted away, haunted by the melody.

Magic crackled along the circle, vibrating in rhythm with the bittersweet wolf song. Adriane sensed her friends' powers forged into one, a ring of protection around her.

She opened her eyes—and she was no longer in

the glade, no longer in Ravenswood. Adriane and Dreamer stood on a twinkling pathway of stars, curving beyond the horizon. The spirit trail.

Its glittering surface flashed bright white, welcoming the warrior and mistwolf. She could sense the generations of wolves who had run this path before her. But there was a loneliness permeating the magical pathway. She felt she might run forever and never find what she was looking for.

"We have your scent, warrior," Dawnrunner spoke in her mind. The wolf stone blazed with power as she felt the circle of protection surge through her, Moonshadow and Dawnrunner guiding her steps.

"Warrior."

Something was calling to her: powerful magic ahead, drawing her forward like a magnet. She moved faster.

On either side of the path, dark shadows flew through the mist, just out of reach.

"Warrior, this way."

A familiar voice echoed across the eerie, shifting magic.

Adriane stopped in her tracks, Dreamer growling at her side. She looked uncertainly into the deep gray fog. What was that? The spirit pack?

"Hurry!" the voice cried out again.

"Tweek?" Adriane asked, astonished.

"You must hurry!" The E. F.'s voice rose in panic.

"Where are you?" The warrior started to step off into the mist.

"Stay on the path," Moonshadow warned.

"Follow me." The Fairimental's voice was closer now. "It's your only chance to save the pack."

Dreamer growled low in his throat, but Adriane pushed past him. She had to risk it; she could feel the magic beckoning her.

She leaped into the gloom. "Tweek?"

The skies exploded with red lightning as the astral planes twisted to murky black.

"Dreamer!" she screamed.

The wolf leaped after her, grabbing hold of her magic.

Adriane tumbled with dizzying speed, losing all sense of time and space.

She landed hard, her shoulder bashing into a jagged rock.

"Dreamer?" she called out, panic washing over her as she looked around.

She was sitting on a wide black rock, mist coiling around her like snakes. Other rocks poked above the surface of a shimmering ocean—not of water, but of magic. In the distance, something rumbled, rising and falling. Huge waves were breaking over a faraway shore.

"Pack mate." Dreamer was behind her, his gleaming white star and paws shining against the dull rock.

She hugged him fiercely. If he hadn't been able to follow her, they could have lost each other.

"Warrior."

A small figure stood in front of her, distorted by a shimmering curtain of mist.

"Tweek?" she asked. "Is that you?"

"Come closer," the E. F. said, his voice sharp and mocking.

Tweek stood before her, red eyes glowing. His mass of ragged sticks and moss stuck out at weird angles. Behind him, shadowy creatures closed in, yellow eyes glittering hungrily.

"Take the mistwolf!" Tweek cackled wildly.

"It's a trap!" Adriane cried.

The creatures lunged. Hideous bat-like demons, their dark, tattered wings carried them across the sparkling sea.

Wolf fire sprung around Adriane and Dreamer in a glowing shield. The beasts shrieked, tearing at her magic with ragged claws. She caught glimpses of bony arms, slitted yellow eyes, and wicked sharp teeth as the bat creatures swarmed, their circle tightening.

Using her magic like a battering ram, she broke through the attackers, sending them scattering.

"Run!" she cried.

Warrior and mistwolf leaped from one rock island to the next. Adriane desperately tried to reach Ravenswood, but she'd severed her connection to the pack when she and Dreamer had left the trail. Now they were lost in the spirit world.

"Dreamer, find the way back!"

"Catch them!" Tweek screamed.

The shrieking creatures charged in a frenzied flapping of wings. Adriane ducked as glittering talons swiped at her from all directions. Golden fire shot from the wolf stone, taking out several demons at once.

Thunder rumbled over the ocean. She looked to the horizon and gasped. A coiling mass of sparkling colors was coming at her, moving across the ocean like a magical tsunami.

Suddenly the creatures dove in, grabbing Dreamer, hoisting him into the air.

Dreamer twisted and growled, trying to break free, but the wolf was outnumbered.

Adriane spun and fired, wolf light exploding from her gem. The demons careened sideways on impact, dropping Dreamer.

"You'll never get out of here!" Tweek yelled.

Adriane leaped and grabbed Tweek, tossing the possessed E. F. to Dreamer. Behind them, she heard wings cutting through the air as the creatures pursued them.

Suddenly an enormous force knocked her feet out from under her. She was pulled down, caught in a riptide as the magic crashed overhead. Strands of blue, green, red, and silver coursed all around her, whipping her through the spirit world with incredible speed. Twisting currents buffeted her back and forth, overwhelming her senses. She was being swept away by wild magic.

She clawed to the surface, relieved to find Dreamer's black head bobbing next to her.

"Dreamer!" she cried as another wave built behind them, surging two stories high. They would be crushed in the roaring magic.

The wolf whined in fear and confusion; wild magic reflected in his wide green eyes. His tracking senses were completely overloaded.

Adriane fired her wolf stone, locking an image in her mind. A surfboard of glowing golden wolf fire formed beneath her. Lying on her stomach, she paddled toward Dreamer. "Hop on!"

Dreamer lunged, Tweek firmly in his jaws, and landed on the front of the board.

The wave crested above their heads and curled, forming a tunnel of swirling ruby, purple, and silver magic.

Placing her right foot forward, Adriane stood, arms out wide, positioning herself for balance. Wolf stone blazing, she surfed through the collapsing wave with lighting speed. She shot out of the imploding tunnel and flew onto another wave of glittering green.

Weaving back and forth, wolf and warrior worked together, trying to sense the pattern of the currents.

Ribbons of brightly colored wild magic swirled, chaotically twisting and smashing together. Crackling bands knotted, forming gleaming riptides that tore through the air in all directions.

"Hang on, Dreamer!"

Adriane pitched right, flying straight up the wave.

Dreamer braced himself as the board shot into the air. At the crest of the wave, Adriane twisted and spun, the board trailing corkscrews of golden fire.

"Are you out of your mind?" Tweek sputtered.

"Put a twig in it!" the warrior shouted.

Struggling to focus, she tried to turn back, but she couldn't fight the immensely powerful current. Her wolf stone flashed in panic. The wild magic could take her anywhere. She'd never find her way home!

Knees bent, she skimmed over the magic swells.

The board flew through the air, narrowly squeezing through two twisting ribbons. Adriane threw her weight to the right, sending the board slicing down the face of another wave.

"Drake. Help me!" She focused with all her will on Drake, hoping the dragon could find them.

Dreamer crouched low, sniffing the flow and eddies of the magic tides.

"That way!" He turned his nose toward a sparkle of light in the distance. A brilliant tower of light shot bright homing beacons in all directions.

"Stone sweet stone!"

Adriane aimed the board straight toward the

Rocking Stone. Catching an orange wave, she rocketed through the astral planes like a golden comet.

"Woohoo!"

Drake's magic wrapped around her like sunlight as she surged forward. Through the swirling white light, she could see a small rounded portal hanging above the Rocking Stone.

Weight centered, knees bent, she went for it.

With a dazzling burst of golden magic, she broke through, soaring high over the glade. Her friends gaped as she flew over their heads.

Staying compact, she leaned back and stomped the landing.

She heard her friends screaming and turned to see why. A wave of demon bats had slipped through, riding the wake of her magic.

Tumbling to the ground, Adriane called out, "Drake, toast them!"

The dragon opened his mouth and roared ferociously—but only a harmless puff of rocky road breath came out.

"What happened to your fire?" Zach asked, firing ruby red bolts of magic to ward off the flying beasts.

"Too much ice cream," Drake groaned, looking at Ozzie.

"What? It was all going to melt." The ferret leaped to the side as dozens of the tattered bats descended on the glade.

Moonshadow howled, a piercing cry that disintegrated several bats instantly; others slammed into the Rocking Stone itself.

"Help the mistwolves!" Adriane cried.

The mages stood together and fired. Wolf, dragon, unicorn, ferret, and healing magic entwined into a lariat of power. Amplified through the mage's jewels, the howl of the wolves hit the bats like dynamite. Wings dissolved into ash as their bodies exploded and fell sizzling into the lake.

"RoooooR!" Tweek wriggled in Dreamer's jaws.

"Quite an entrance," Kara said, unicorn jewel blazing diamond bright.

"What's happened to Tweek?" Emily ran forward, taking the twitching, screaming E. F. from the mistwolf's mouth.

"He's under the spell of the Spider Witch," Adriane said to the healer.

"Are you all right?" Zach asked Adriane.

"I'm fine, thanks to you guys," Adriane told them.

"*I found you,*" Drake said, wrapping his giant wings around Adriane.

"Thank you." Adriane hugged his scaly chest, then turned to her friends. "I didn't find Storm."

"What about the power crystal?" Kara asked.

"Wild magic swept me away before I could look for it."

"Take the mistwolf!" Tweek screamed.

"Ahhh!" Ozzie ducked as bolts of red magic shot from Tweek's gem.

"I can't get through to him!" Emily struggled with the Fairimental's flailing twigs.

"He's tweeking out." Raising her unicorn jewel, Kara encased the possessed E. F. in a sphere of white and pink magic.

"Maybe you can help him," Emily said to Adriane. "You're both tuned to earth magic."

Tweek thrashed wildly inside the bubble. "I'll destroy you all!"

The warrior shrugged. "Well, he couldn't get much worse."

Dreamer, Moonshadow, and Dawnrunner took position by the warrior's side; Drake and the rest of the mistwolves behind her.

Steeling herself, Adriane drew on the strength of her friends and focused on Tweek's glowing red HORARFF.

She concentrated on the healing magic Emily had given her as golden fire swirled into the glowing red.

Suddenly she sensed another layer to the magic, made up of the deep green of trees, the velvety brown of bark, the sparkling blue of spring flowers—all the vitality and strength of the forest.

She thought of Orenda, and her wolf stone glowed brighter, gold edged with silver and green. Tweek reached to her, climbing out of the darkness and latching on to Adriane's pure magic.

The E. F. stood before them, quartz eyes whirling with golden magic, HORARFF shining bright turquoise.

"Speak to me, Twighead," Ozzie pleaded.

The little Fairimental looked over his twiggy arms and legs, then stared at the ferret. "Inconceivable!"

"You did it!" Emily cried, as Kara and Zach high-fived the warrior.

Tweek shook his twigs and leaves back to a semblance of his earthly body.

"Tweek, what happened to you?" Emily asked, smoothing a section of moss on his head.

Quartz eyes twinkled, focusing on the mages. "The very magic that holds me together was twisted. Disgusting!"

"Just like the forest spirit," Adriane realized.

"The spirit world is completely flooey! There's wild magic all over the place."

"I noticed." Adriane leaned against Drake's soft neck as she caught her breath. The dragon's large head hung over her shoulder, covering her protectively. "Maybe the spirit pack got swept away on the wild magic, like I did."

"*Possible,*" Moonshadow agreed.

"Tweek, what is the Spider Witch doing?" Emily asked.

"She had me release all those . . . things to try to take Dreamer."

"What were they?" Zach asked.

"Dark creatures that live in the astral planes."

Tweek twirled about. "What concerns me is the fact she could twist Fairimental magic at all!"

"Hold up," Kara said. "What about the forest spirit?"

Tweek looked at his HORARFF. "I'm afraid it's going to transform into something horrible."

"What do we do now?" Zach asked.

Tweek straightened his twigs and marched forward. "We study and decipher mysterious, ancient symbols."

Ozzie rolled his eyes, laughing. "You kill me, Twighead."

"No, look."

Everyone turned around and gasped. The Rocking Stone pulsed with bright white magic, ablaze with glowing symbols.

Chapter 11

"**W**ow, look at this." Zach walked around the base of the towering Rocking Stone.

Symbols pulsed in sequence like glowing hiero-glyphics.

"Good gak!" Tweek studied scrolling bytes of data projected from his HORARFF, trying to find a match.

"The Rocking Stone is an ancient Indian totem. I looked it up on the Web," Emily said. "Legends call it a spirit door."

"I flew through it escaping the astral planes," Adriane said.

"Precisely." Tweek continued scrolling through data. "This stone is a place where the real world and the astral planes intersect. My guess is, this is how the witch has infiltrated the glade with her weaving."

"How do we close it?" Adriane asked.

"You can't," Tweek continued. "But you must have activated these markings when you broke through."

"Good job," Zach told the warrior, smiling.

"Yeah, if I knew what I did, it'd be great."

"It seems to be some kind of message," Tweek concluded.

"From who?" Ozzie asked.

"I don't know," the Experimental Fairimental conceded.

"What's it say?" Ozzie persisted.

"I don't know."

"What's the capital of Arizona?!"

"I don't know."

"Ozzie," Emily said, pulling the agitated ferret back. "Let him work."

Tweek scanned his light over the markings. "I think the message has to do with using elemental magic."

"Hey, look." Kara pointed to a symbol of curling flames glowing orange, red, and yellow on the stone's surface. "There's me, fire."

"Yes," Tweek observed, "and this is water, air, earth, and . . . what the—"

Zach's ruby dragon stone gleamed as he ran it over a strange circular symbol with a lopsided triangle. "What is that?"

"Pizza?" Ozzie guessed, squinting at the stone.

"Step aside." Tweek projected a huge magnifying glass and studied the strange symbol. "Hmmm, I don't know about this one."

"Tweek," Emily said. "Adriane helped fix your magic."

"Thank you," the E. F. mumbled.

Kara looked at the darkening glade. "If Adriane healed you, could we use the same magic to heal Orenda?"

"Theoretically. But I'm just a mass of earthly matter," Tweek said. "The forest sylph is an ancient fairy creature, connected to every tree and plant in this forest."

"We have to try," Adriane said.

"No, no, no!" Tweek protested. "My basic elements are tied to earth, like the forest spirit, so I'm susceptible. But so are Adriane and the mistwolves. Orenda is trapped in a powerful weaving. You'd have to be fully trained in elemental magic to protect yourselves against that spell, let alone reverse it."

"Mistwolves are not afraid," Moonshadow growled.

Dawnrunner stood by her mate, eyes glinting fire. *"Better we try than watch our pups grow without magic."*

Adriane thought of the raging magic pulling at her. The same thing was happening to the mistwolves. When their magic disappeared, they would be plain wolves, pure savage animals. What would happen to her?

Dreamer whined low, feeling the warrior's fear.

"Using elemental magic before you're ready is extremely dangerous. Look what happened to the Spider Witch," Tweek said.

Kara shuddered. "You mean she's, like, a spider?"

Tweek nodded. "The transformation gave her

remarkable powers to weave elemental magic, but she is no longer a fairy creature."

The wind howled through the glade, an eerie sound, almost as if the trees were crying.

Kara turned to the group of mages and animals. "There *is* magic powerful enough to save Ravenswood and the mistwolves."

"The power crystal." Adriane clenched her hand into a fist.

"It worked in the Fairy Realms," Kara concluded.

"Forget it," Tweek barked at Adriane. "You were nearly lost in the astral planes. And you!" His eyes spun colors as he turned to Kara. "What makes you think you can handle that kind of power? You already destroyed one."

"It was an accident," Kara said.

"We don't have a choice!" Adriane cried as thunder suddenly rocked the skies. Storm clouds gathered overhead, a dense mass silhouetting the trees in a seething darkness.

"There's isn't much time left." Kara indicated the drooping, graying branches. "If those demons are any indication of what to expect, we have to try!"

"The Spider Witch is only getting more powerful." Adriane's voice rose, her black eyes sparking as she stood firm beside Dreamer. "I say we strike now, when she's not expecting it. It's the only advantage we've got."

"*I agree with the mages,*" Moonshadow said.

"We must find the power crystal," Dawnrunner added emphatically.

Tweek saw the determination on the faces around him. "I will say this: I have never met mages like you before." His body rattled as a few mounds of moss slipped to the grass. "Of course, I never met *anyone* before you."

Moonshadow snarled at the twiggy figure.

"Oh, all right." Tweek hoisted his twigs into place. "First, you need to know a few rules about Level Two mageing."

"Right," Kara agreed.

"Level Two mages must have"—he held up twiggy fingers and counted off—"a tuned jewel."

"Check," Adriane, Kara, Emily, Ozzie, and Zach said.

"At least one bonded magical animal."

"Check," Adriane, Kara, and Zach echoed.

"*And* an elemental paladin."

"Here," Kara responded, looking at the others.

"It's too risky!" Twigs went flying as Tweek cartwheeled about. "You're all over the map!"

"We need to figure out what elements we are," Zach said, studying the markings.

"Who are you, anyway?" Tweek's quartz eyes rolled in his twigs.

"That's Zach, another mage, and my baby boy, Drake," Adriane said.

"BaaWoW, the Drake is famous among Fairimentals!" Tweek exclaimed, then sighed. "Okay, well, we know Kara is fire."

Adriane swung her wolf stone. Gold and red sparks trailed over the stone's surface. A tree wrapped in ivy crackled with green and deep gold against the granite.

"Earth, naturally," Tweek said.

Emily stepped up, passing her rainbow stone over the glowing symbols. A series of cresting wave markings flashed aquamarine and diamond white.

"Emily is water," Tweek said.

"Lemme see that thing!" Ozzie stomped over, nose to rock, scanning the jewel on his collar. Several bright puffy clouds flashed on the stone, edged in gleaming silver.

"Ozzie's definitely full of hot air," Kara remarked.

"Thank you." Ozzie proudly polished his jewel with his furry arm.

"We need room," Tweek said as he wobbled to the lake in the center of the glade.

The mages followed the E. F. expectantly.

"Everyone stand with your bonded animals," he instructed.

Adriane stood with the mistwolves, Kara with Lyra, and Zach with Drake. Ozzie took a step toward Emily.

"Hey! You're an elf, and a mage, too—sort of," Tweek reminded him. "And neither of you have bonded with an animal."

"Maybe Ozzie bonded with himself," Kara suggested.

"That's ridiculous." Ozzie looked himself over, smoothing his cowlick.

"Not everyone is meant for Level Two," the E. F. advised. "Kara happens to have the perfect combination of magic. She is a blazing star tuned to a unicorn jewel, bonded to Lyra *and* a firemental stallion."

"Perfect," Kara mouthed as she coyly twirled her sparkling jewel.

"Wait," Adriane said. "So if the Spider Witch is an elemental master, then she has a paladin, too?"

"I bet it's that big creepy spider I saw in her lair." Kara shuddered.

"Yes . . . ," Tweek said, eyes popping. "If there was a way to get rid of her paladin, we could weaken her powers—"

"*And* her hold on Ravenswood!" Ozzie finished.

"We don't have time to break into her lair!" Adriane insisted. "We have to heal Orenda now!"

"But there's only one of us who is a Level Two mage," Emily said.

"I can boost the rest of you," Kara suggested. "That's what a blazing star does. Uses magic to help everyone else."

Adriane gave Kara a nod and stepped to a line of trees near the lake's edge. "She's somewhere around here."

"Let's kick it." Kara held up her unicorn jewel, swirling diamond magic around her arms.

"O' me twig," Tweek sputtered.

The blazing star concentrated, morphing her magic into red, pink, and orange flames. With a wave of her hands, she pulled the fire together, letting it mix with the amber glow of the wolf stone.

Amplified by Kara's magic, Adriane whipped golden fire around four of the nearest trees. She immediately felt a jolt. The trees were trying to fight the strangling power of the weaving.

"I can feel the webs!" Adriane tried to pull the dark magic away, but couldn't.

Ozzie focused on his stone. "Air—what does that mean, Tweekster?"

"Could be levitation, wind . . ."

Ozzie looked to Kara. His gem glowed bright amber. Then a burst of wind shot from his stone, throwing the ferret backward. He tumbled head over heels into the lake.

"Very good," Tweek commented.

Emily focused on the lake, trying to pull the flailing ferret back to shore. Her rainbow stone shone blue, green, and purple as she bore down harder. The lake surface rippled slightly.

"Kara, give me a boost," she instructed.

Kara draped the healer in pink and white diamond twinkles. A wave surged across the lake, delivering the soggy ferret onto the bank with a splatter.

Adriane's magic sparked. Waves of fire leaped into the air and vanished, leaving the trees untouched.

"This is so not working." The warrior put her stone down, exhausted and disappointed.

Moonshadow gathered the pack around the warrior. *"Try again."*

Focusing, the warrior reached into the earth, feeling dark magic running through the roots. The weaving sapped at her bright fire, swallowing its power. But deep underneath she felt something, a spark of life. Opening herself to the mistwolves, she snarled and grabbed the earth magic.

Tweek went flying across the glade and smashed into the Rocking Stone, releasing a burst of dirt. "Aggooy."

Adriane felt her magic drain away with the effort.

The E. F. spun to his feet, tumbling his way back to the glade. "Yes, well, although she doesn't have a paladin, the pull of the mistwolves is very strong."

All the animals of Ravenswood had now gathered in the glade to help.

"Teamwork, people!" Kara held up her shining unicorn jewel, sending rings of pale orange fire to encircle the trees.

The others held up their gems, concentrating. Blue, green, red, gold, and amber sparkled along Kara's swirling firemental magic.

"Careful," the blazing star cautioned. "Okay, let's take it out."

The circle of magic spread slowly outward, covering several dozen more trees.

"Easy . . . okay." The blazing star nodded to the warrior.

With the mistwolves supporting her, Adriane reached frantically, trying to stop the poison from spreading. But the circle of fire washed harmlessly across the glade.

Mistwolves growled, snapping at the air in frustration.

"That was . . . something," Tweek said.

The mages exchanged anxious glances, their jewels lowered and lifeless.

"Great, now what?" Kara asked.

"If only I knew how to use the magic better," Zach muttered, frustrated.

"If only we could contact the Fairimentals, or the unicorns," Emily said worriedly.

"We don't have enough time to practice!" Kara threw her hands in the air.

A feeling of despondency and hopelessness hung heavy in the air.

"We suck!" a quiffle squeaked.

"You made it worse," Adriane accused Kara.

"I did not!" Kara faced the warrior.

"Did."

"Not!" Kara said to Adriane. "You're doing it wrong."

"I am not!"

"*I'm* the one here with Level Two magic!" Kara yelled.

"Oh, if you're so perfect"—Adriane got right in Kara's face—"why don't you just save the preserve yourself?"

"Maybe I will!"

"We're doomed!" Rasha cried.

KAooOOGAH!

Everyone jumped, startled by a booming blast from the ferret stone.

Ozzie marched to the front of the group, determination shining in his eyes, and began speaking in a loud, clear voice. "Listen up! I may be a ferret but—"

"You're an elf," Tweek corrected him.

"I may be an elf, but—"

"He's an elf?" a startled quiffle asked.

"You look like a ferret," a mistwolf observed.

"GaH!"

"Quiet!" Emily demanded.

"It doesn't matter what we are," Ozzie continued. "The Dark Sorceress and the Spider Witch are back and more dangerous than ever. Wild magic is flooeying all over the place. Our home is in danger—"

A few quiffles and brimbees started crying.

"Gah! The only way we're going to succeed is if we work together." He walked to a quivering quiffle, lifting its beak.

"It doesn't matter that we can't even make a simple magic . . . er, thing."

He turned to a brimbee. "When the Dark Sorceress blew up the whatever-that-was, did we back down?"

"No!" the group answered.

Ozzie challenged the mistwolves. "When the mistwolves were trapped, did Stormbringer let them down?"

"No!" Adriane yelled.

"That's right! So are we going to give up when Ravenswood needs us?"

The resounding "No!" echoed throughout the glade.

"Whatever the Spider Witch has planned, whether it's disgusting webs, incredibly powerful elemental magic, giant fanged spiders—"

"Whoa."

"Whatever comes, it just doesn't matter!" the ferret shouted. "We are going to work together and save Ravenswood!"

"Yay!" everyone cheered wildly.

"It's time!" Tweek screamed.

"Let's go!" Ozzie yelled, frizzled hair sticking straight out.

"No, it's *time!*" Tweek's twigs rattled as he found a match for Zach's mysterious symbol on the Rocking Stone. "Zach is *time,* a fifth element!"

"What does that mean?" the boy asked.

"You are the anchor, the one who keeps all the other elements rooted here in the real world," Tweek explained.

"Like the circle of protection." Dreamer understood.

"Exactly," Tweek agreed. "With the dragon, you can hold Adriane steady—well, *steadier,* if she goes back in."

Adriane clasped Zach's hands in hers. "You mean *when* I go back in."

"I won't let you get lost again," Zach vowed.

Adriane smiled and nodded. "Okay, here's the play," she said, addressing the group. "Dreamer and I are going back. We'll find Storm, and together we'll find the spirit pack."

The mistwolves howled in a chorus of agreement.

"The magic of the spirit pack will help attract the power crystal," the warrior declared, turning to the blazing star.

"Yeah, that should do it," Kara concurred.

"Dreamer will bring it back," Zach agreed.

"And we'll use the power crystal to heal the forest sylph," Emily concluded.

A cacophony of cheers meant all the animals were down with the brave plan.

Time was running out. Adriane hoped Ozzie was right and that their determination would be enough. It was all they had.

Chapter 12

The Dark Sorceress edged aside as spiders skittered into the thick mist.

The giant tapestry crackled as the Spider Witch's bulky robed form moved back and forth, conducting the hundreds of spiders busily weaving the final details.

The time for patience is almost at an end, the sorceress told herself. The source of her ally's power would soon reveal itself, and when it did, the sorceress would strike.

She stepped back as a giant spider descended out of the mist.

The Spider Witch laughed, stroking the spider's spiky head.

"I know what you are thinking," the witch said slowly, her voice low and threatening. "Your elemental transformation was never complete. There is a part of you still human, and that will always be your weakness."

"You have the power here, not me." The sorceress bowed her head in subservience.

"Serve me and I can complete your magic."

The sorceress's animal eyes flashed.

"Or I could feed you to my hungry friend."

Clattering mandibles clicked an eerie staccato as the spider watched the sorceress coldly.

"I would prefer the former," the sorceress conceded.

"Then I think you'll like this final touch."

The spider moved away, golden thread trailing from its swollen abdomen. The witch raised her hand. A ruby gem gleamed powerfully on her finger. With a quick slash, she cut the final strand with a sharp fingernail.

The entire tapestry shifted, rippling like a reflection in a pool. Silken threads quivered as the building magic writhed through the design. A sudden gust of wind surged through the chamber, carrying the crisp scent of ancient forest. High, keening wolf howls leaked from the swirling patterns.

The sorceress's skin prickled—the weaving was coming to life!

The Spider Witch cackled gleefully. "Watch and learn what a magic master can do."

It was as if they stood high above Ravenswood, looking down. The details were amazing, every tree, every blade of grass, the woodland trails, blue streams running into lakes, the intricate details of the sculpture gardens, topiary animals, Ravenswood Manor itself. And in the center—the magic glade, the heart of the forest.

The witch waved her hand, and the glade zoomed forward, magnifying every secret in exquisite detail.

"All is ready."

    ❧   ❧   ❧

The shining spirit trail stretched before Adriane and Dreamer.

She couldn't hear her friends through the layers of swirling magic but she could feel them. Tweek had been right: Dragon magic was as ancient as time itself, and it was Drake and Zach now keeping her steady. With Dreamer guiding her, she kept on the path.

Wild magic swells rose and fell to the sides, attracted to the wolf stone and mistwolf, brilliant spray breaking upon the trail's edge.

A sudden feeling of loss stopped her. Emptiness, like cold rain, swept over her. She felt alone, all her fears and memories bubbling to the surface. But this time, instead of pulling away, she reached for them, allowing the jagged feelings of isolation and sadness to fill her with frozen dread.

She took a deep breath. "Here," she said calmly. "This is where it happened."

The black mistwolf trotted to her side. *"The spirit pack was taken here."*

Adriane stood in the middle of the spirit trail, the future ahead, past behind. She closed her eyes and focused, letting wolf magic flow through her. Blues mixed with swaths of white and green swirled in her head. Her nose filled with the extraordinary scents of wood, loam, and wildflowers. Her heart raced with the devotion and love of her pack mates. She pressed on, trying to see through Storm's eyes, feeling what Storm was feeling—and reached for her lost friend.

The shift was slight, barely perceptible.

Through a warm haze, Adriane saw herself. She was standing on a grassy hill, eyes closed, arms outstretched.

She opened her eyes and looked in wonder. The forests of Ravenswood spread miles in every direction, a vast ocean of greens and browns sparkling under skies of blue and white.

But it was not the shock of being back in Ravenswood that made her gasp. In front of her, not ten feet away, stood a lone mistwolf. Her silver-and-white fur gleamed with magic, golden eyes shining.

"Storm!"

Without thinking, Adriane raced to her friend. The large wolf reared up to place her paws on her pack mate's shoulders in a wolfish embrace.

Adriane had never felt such joy. She howled with pleasure, jumping and leaping, rolling on the ground just as they once had.

Atop the rolling hills, amid the wildflowers and tall, sweet grass, Storm lay beside Adriane, golden eyes glinting with light. Together, they looked out upon the forests they both loved.

"Storm, I can't believe it's really you." Adriane

threw her arms around her friend, burying her face in warm, silvery fur. "I never want to leave here, ever!"

"I wish that could be, Adriane," Stormbringer answered.

"So much has happened, I . . . I . . ." She was about to introduce Storm to Dreamer when she realized the black mistwolf was nowhere to be found.

"The mistwolves are in terrible danger."

Suddenly, the silver wolf's form wavered, dissipating to mist, before weaving back.

Adriane scrambled to her feet, panic shooting through her.

"Storm, what's wrong?" Adriane asked nervously.

"I must return to the spirit world."

"Aren't we there now?"

"This is only a dream state."

Only a dream. But it felt so real, so alive.

"Will you come with me, warrior? See me as I really am."

"I know who you really are," Adriane said, bracing herself. "Take me with you."

Storm nodded, closing her golden eyes briefly. Her fur shone like moonlight.

In a swirling wash of greens and browns, the forest melted away.

A sudden rush of sound thundered like the crash of a cannon. Dust filled Adriane's eyes and throat.

The scene before her was one of total chaos, a cacophony of noise and confusion. Huge slabs of rock crashed to the floor. Adriane staggered as the walls of an underground chamber fell around her.

Adriane had been plunged into the middle of her nightmare: Her pack mate was trapped, and she was helpless to do anything about it.

In the center of the chamber, the last of the sorceress's crystals splintered and cracked as it filled with waves of magic from Avalon. The Dark Sorceress had trapped the mistwolves in immense crystals, using the wolves to attract the magic of Avalon. Storm stood, wavering in and out of mist as she helped the last of the mistwolves leap free of the death trap.

Across the vast chamber Adriane heard her friends desperately calling to her. Kara, Emily, and Zach tried to reach her, but instead she ran toward her struggling pack mate. She would never let her down. Golden wolf fire sprang from the wolf stone spiraling toward her friend. The magic locked around the fading mistwolf.

"Do not let go."

"Never!" With every fiber of her being, Adriane held on to Storm. The world turned upside down as Adriane was swept through an endless forest, wordless memories of sorrow and passion filling her senses.

Time crashed to a stop.

Adriane stood at the edge of a high cliff. Silver rocks glittered, leading from the ledge to the sprawling drop far below. A stream of mist bridged the chasm, stretching over a river of raging wild magic. Ribbons of brilliant blue, purple, red, and silver thrashed in the narrow gap, surging upward, flowing in a fast river.

"I knew you would find me."

Storm's voice echoed in her mind, but the silver wolf was nowhere to be seen.

On the far side of the chasm, Adriane could see the glistening lines of the spirit trail. The end of the misty bridge entwined with the glowing lines, fading away in the distance. A bolt of crackling magic burst from the river below, shredding a section of mist to fragments.

Adriane's wolf stone blazed with danger as pain tore through her, as if a part of her were being ripped to shreds.

She fought to stand strong. "Storm, where are you?"

"I am here." Storm's disembodied voice echoed in the wide space.

Adriane looked at the bridge of mist and gasped.

The section of spirit trail stretching over the chasm had been destroyed. Now only Storm's mist united the two sides, keeping the trail whole. Once her mist faded, the entire spirit trail would collapse, and the memories and magic of the mistwolves would vanish into nothingness, lost forever.

"I cannot hold on much longer," the mistwolf said, her voice strained.

"What's happened to you?"

"I am holding the last of the mistwolves' magic."

Adriane looked around desperately. "Where is the rest of the spirit pack?"

"They are lost. You must find them."

"I don't understand," Adriane said. "If the spirit pack was swept away by the wild magic, why weren't you taken with them?"

"I ran with the spirit pack, but I was never part of them."

Adriane was unable to speak. The realization rocked her to the very core of her being.

"I was swept onto the trail from the Dark Sorceress' lair, but I have remained here in mist form."

"But why didn't you tell me?" Adriane asked, tears running down her cheeks. "I could have helped."

"You did. You have held me in your dreams."

Adriane flashed on the dark dreams that had haunted her since she lost Storm—her desperate attempts to hold on to her friend, to keep her from slipping away. "I thought they were nightmares," she whispered, horrified. "I didn't know."

Storm's mist wavered, nearly disintegrating before pulling back together.

Fear tingled up and down Adriane's spine. Storm

had replaced the spirit pack, holding the mistwolves of Aldenmor from losing their magic. And that meant if Adriane could find the missing pack in time, she could bring Storm back with her—alive!

Adriane fought to remain calm. There wasn't much time. She had been given a second chance, and she wasn't going to waste it. But only the magic of Avalon itself could help her.

"I have to find the power crystal."

Suddenly a tremor shook the chasm, and the wild magic exploded. A shock wave surged through the air, sending Adriane tumbling through walls of vibrant color.

"No!"

It was too late.

She felt the magic of her friends take hold and drag her from the spirit world, Storm's mist vanishing before her eyes.

She heard the sounds of yelling as magic flashed everywhere.

"Adriane!"

Zach ran toward her. "Are you all right?

"I . . . don't know." She stood in the glade, watching the scene as if this, too, were a dream.

"We're under attack!" Kara yelled.

Sudden pain lashed through her, making her cry out. She saw Emily and Kara, magic blazing from their jewels. The mistwolves ran about the glade, trying to contain the dark forces that had finally broken through. Trees sagged into the water, their flowing branches weighed down by glistening spiderwebs. And in the center of a clump of willows, suspended by twisted hunks of spiderwebbing, hung the sickly, green cocoon. Blistered with pockmarks, the thing pulsed, tearing wicked cracks up and down. The vile apparition shuddered, ready to unleash the demon inside.

"The webs appeared out of nowhere!" Emily cried, running to Adriane's side as she fired intense volleys of healing magic.

Adriane tried to add her magic to that of her friends, but all she felt was the agony of the forest sylph.

Adriane ignored the intense emotions bombarding her and searched for the one who could help her most.

"Dreamer?" she called out desperately.

But Dreamer was gone.

Chapter 13

In a flash of bloodred light, heavy webbing exploded over the glade as the cocoon burst open. Adriane felt the world spinning, twisting her stomach in a knot. Wolf stone sparking, she looked around frantically for Orenda, but all that remained was a mass of strands coiling over the trees. Whatever was in the cocoon had disappeared.

The mistwolves leaped through the glade, snarling as they searched for the forest sylph.

The healer rushed toward Adriane, red curls tumbling wildly over her sweat-streaked face.

"Emily," Adriane whispered, dark eyes shining. "She's alive."

"Who?" Kara raced over, Lyra landing beside her.

"Stormbringer."

Emily and Kara gasped.

Adriane turned to Moonshadow and Dawnrunner. "She's been trapped in mist form ever since she saved the mistwolves from the sorceress."

"Storm is the one holding us to the spirit trail," Moonshadow realized, his eyes glinting with feral light.

"I have to go back before it's too late," Adriane said. "Dreamer's still there."

Dawnrunner addressed the pack. *"No one gets left behind."*

The mistwolves howled as everyone gathered behind Adriane.

"We have to stop that sylph!" Tweek rattled atop Ariel's back as the owl landed. "If she takes the magic of Ravenswood to the spirit world, she's going to get the power crystal."

"Where did she go?" Kara nervously asked.

Wind screamed through the forest, tangling the remaining webs draped in the trees.

"That way." The warrior pointed toward broken branches and downed trunks littering the forest floor.

"I can smell the foul thing," Moonshadow confirmed.

The group moved cautiously to the edge of the glade, following the trail of destruction.

"Tweek, where is it?" Adriane asked, eyes narrowed, jewel held high as she swept a beam of magical light over the surrounding trees.

Tweek stretched his twigs out like antennae, pointing to a giant fir. "O' me, me, me—"

"Keep your twigs together, man!" Ozzie shouted.

"TWI—!" Tweek exploded in a burst of mud and sticks.

With a wrenching *crack,* the tree trunk split, spewing red light across the ground. The mutated forest sylph emerged.

"Orenda!" Adriane gasped as the demon's twisted magic slammed into her.

The sylph had been monstrously transformed. Red eyes glowing from its shifting, translucent form, the nightmarish thing floated in the air. Root legs like spider limbs reached out. Crooked needle fingers grew from bent limbs. The sylph's once beautiful features were wracked by livid scars, pulling her mouth into a malicious grin.

Adriane's tears felt like fire on her face.

"Warrior," the demon sneered, expanding its ghostly form. Leaves, branches, and pieces of earth flew toward it like a powerful magnet. "You have nothing left."

The magic of Ravenswood swirled inside the vengeful spirit, pure green and gold warping to red. Adriane's wolf stone erupted in a shower of red sparks.

Zach and Kara fired their jewels, slamming dragon and unicorn magic into the thing.

The demon roared, gathered its thrashing roots, and plunged into another tree. Bolts of energy raced through the trunk as the demon fed on the tree's earth magic.

Adriane doubled over as the screams of the trees burned through the wolf stone.

Golden magic shimmering along their lustrous fur, Dawnrunner and five wolves lunged at the infected tree. Shrieking at the touch of the wolves' pure magic, the demon zipped out, disappearing into the next tree.

Struggling as her gem flickered between red and gold, Adriane fought the demon's pull. Her friends were firing volleys of magic, but without her earth elemental magic, they could not heal Orenda.

The demon shot from the glade into the depths of the forest, devouring everything in its path.

"What do we do?" Kara shouted, unicorn jewel sparking in her hand. "Can we heal Orenda, turn her back?"

"We have to get her in one place long enough to find out," Emily responded.

"We need to set a trap," Adriane said.

"What's the bait?" Zach asked.

"We give it what it wants." Adriane held up her wrist, wolf stone pulsing with light.

"That's crazy!" Kara cried.

"No way!" Emily protested.

Adriane faced her friends. "*I'm* the one attuned to earth magic."

"It's too dangerous," Ozzie exclaimed. "What if that only makes the demon stronger?"

"We have to try." Before the others could talk her out of it, she quickly continued. "We need a distraction."

Zach swung onto Drake's back. "Leave *that* to us."

"Lyra, follow Orenda!" Kara ordered.

The cat gave Ozzie a flick of her head.

"Doh!" The ferret reluctantly climbed aboard. "I really hate flying."

The cat's golden wings shimmered and unfolded as she soared upward, Ozzie hanging on.

"Moonshadow, try to herd it away from the deep forest," Adriane ordered.

The black wolf started barking orders. *"I want four groups led by Dawnrunner, Whitefang, Comet, and Aja."*

"I will go with Adriane." Dawnrunner stepped between Moonshadow and the warrior.

Moonshadow stood nose to nose with his mate. A spark flashed between their eyes as the pack leader submitted and padded to the other wolves.

"We'll meet in back of the manor," Adriane continued. "Good luck."

A flaming maple tree shot into the air like a rocket, streaking across the sky as it disintegrated into embers.

"The demon is making its way through Turtle Bog!" Ozzie reported from high atop Lyra.

Moonshadow bounded into the woods. The rest of the wolves raced after him.

Adriane ran her hand over Drake's neck, feeling the dragon's strength. "Be careful," she said to Zach.

"Let's fly!" Drake snorted fire. With a beat of enormous wings, dragon and rider took to the skies.

Healer, blazing star, warrior, and mistwolf took off toward the manor.

Drake and Zach sliced through the sky, swooping in as the poisoned sylph burrowed through a line of pine trees.

Howling their battle cry, mistwolves forced the demon across a grassy clearing to the topiary garden on the eastern hills of the preserve.

In a blaze of red dust, Orenda shot down a slope and engulfed a topiary brontosaurus.

The green dinosaur sculpture flashed red—and came to life. It swung a massive tail at the wolves. But Moonshadow bore down from the west, snarling and ripping at the dino's haunches. A blast of dragon fire from the skies smacked into the bronto, forcing the demon to jump into the tyrannosaurus topiary. The huge shrub sculpture shuddered, its neatly shorn leaves crackling and glowing red as it thundered toward the dragon. Zach and Drake rounded on the T rex, encasing it with pure ruby dragon magic. The demon dino dodged aside, sinking glowing red teeth into Drake's tail. The dragon bellowed, tail smoking.

"Drake!" Adriane cried, feeling the dragon's pain.

"Come on, we have to hurry while it's distracted," Kara called, running past the mermaid fountain in the water gardens.

Emily slipped a steadying arm through the warrior's as they followed Kara and Dawnrunner across the great lawns. They came to a stop at the forest's edge.

"Which one?" Emily asked, scanning the magnificent trees bordering the lawn.

Adriane had to choose. She stopped in front of a giant oak. Its immense trunk rose into a mass of branches thick with green leaves.

"You must ask the tree to help us," Dawnrunner urged.

Adriane placed her hands on the tree trunk, the bark rough against her palms. She closed her eyes and concentrated. Magic tingled up and down her arms. She could feel the gnarled roots draw strength from the land. She reached farther, touching another tree, then another. With love and patience, Orenda had woven each tree into an intricate network, nurturing the natural magic of Ravenswood.

"Great tree," Adriane spoke quietly. "Orenda has given so much to make you strong and healthy. Please, help her now."

The tree groaned and creaked. Adriane winced. She thought she heard the entire forest scream with the agony of the demon's attack.

"I'm sorry," Adriane whispered to the oak. "Please help us."

As if acknowledging the warrior's presence, the tree seemed to calm.

Wolf stone shining, Adriane sent earth magic into

the tree. The healer and blazing star added their magic, entwining blues, pinks, and whites into the wolf stone. Adriane directed the flow of power through the trunk, into every root and every branch. The leaves glowed with swirling colors.

"We stand with you," she told the tree as the magic shone into the sky like a beacon.

On the other side of the preserve, the dino-tope turned, attracted by the vibrant magic. With a withering red flash, the demon zipped away from its host. The enormous scorched-leaf sculpture stood suspended for one precarious moment before crashing to the ground, crushing a triceratops topiary.

"*Heads up!*" Lyra soared over the mages.

"It's coming!" Ozzie yelled, arms flailing. "Right toward you!"

The red glow of the demon filtered through the trees like an unnatural sunset.

Eyes blazing, it streaked across the lawn.

Dawnrunner turned to face the oncoming monster.

Kara and Emily took position on either side of the tree, jewels raised.

"Steady." Adriane breathed deeply, struggling to contain the magic roiling inside the tree.

The haggard wolves fanned out in a U shape, Drake zooming overhead, guiding the demon as it headed straight for the huge oak—and Adriane.

With a fierce snarl, Dawnrunner crouched low, magic crackling along her coat.

"Dawnrunner!" Adriane cried.

"Stand strong, warrior." The wolf held her ground, sending her magic not to defend herself from the demon—but to protect Adriane.

The demon collided with Dawnrunner in a sickening rush. For a split second, wolf and demon merged, exploding in a blaze of fire. Waves of twisted magic crashed over Adriane as the demon leaped into the glowing tree.

She saw Dawnrunner's limp body sprawled across the ashen ground. Once again a wolf had sacrificed herself and Adriane hadn't been able to stop it.

Emily ran to the downed wolf, healing stone blazing.

Keening howls sliced over the preserve as the wolves sensed the loss of their fallen pack mate.

Adriane felt the evil spirit meld with the tree, sinking its venom into the rich veins. She grabbed at the demon, twisting her magic around it like a rope. Dawnrunner's brave act had weakened the creature.

The warrior held up her jewel and met Moonshadow's steely eyes.

"Fire!" Adriane ordered.

Five jewels erupted with magic, encasing the tree in a glittering force field. The wolves surrounded the tree, giving all they had left to help the mages.

The demon shrieked, thrashing the oak's wide branches.

"Orenda, come back to us." The warrior flattened

her palms on the tree, moving tendrils of golden magic into the demon.

The contact burned like fire. She could feel the energy of Ravenswood pulsing through the demon as the Spider Witch threaded each tree into her horrible spell.

Tweek's magic had felt like this at first, too, all swirling and dark, but she had found the pure elemental spark within him. She focused harder, desperately trying to touch the gentle forest sylph.

But Orenda was being controlled like a puppet, forced to destroy everything she had spent years building.

Adriane cried out. No trace of Orenda's pure blue, gold, and green magic remained. Utter blackness had consumed the sylph. The witch had wormed her way into the heart of Ravenswood and extinguished its light—Orenda was no more.

"It's too late." The warrior slumped to the ground, eyes glazed with tears. Once again, she had failed.

"Keep firing!" Kara's jewel blazed with red, pink, and white fire.

The trapped demon shrieked in anger as the force field closed around it.

There was only one place the demon could go now—and there was only one thing left for Adriane to do.

The warrior rose, eyes sparking. Magic crashed through her, but it didn't matter. Rage and sorrow burned inside. The mistwolves had come to her for help, to make their stand. Now Dawnrunner had paid for that trust. Chain's words rang in her head, mocking her. How many more would suffer before this was over? How many more would she betray?

This was her fault. She had to make it right.

With all the strength she had left, she reached out and grabbed the demon, tightening her golden wolf magic around its very core.

"Adriane!" Emily's cry drifted away.

Brilliant dragon magic reached out to her, but she ignored it.

"Where is she?" Zach's worried voice floated from a million miles away.

The faint cries of her friends faded as she fell.

Chain's wolfish laughter echoed ahead of her in the swirling gloom.

Then everything went black as Adriane plummeted into the oblivion between worlds.

Chapter 14

Her feet hit solid ground, crunching the thick layer of leaves and twigs on the forest floor.

What happened? Was she still in Ravenswood?

She turned. A stand of oaks was behind her. One of the trees had an ornately carved door leading right into it.

That's very curious, she thought.

She opened the door and cautiously stepped inside. Following a long, winding tunnel, she finally emerged in a strange garden. Giant flowers bloomed beside golden geometric hedges.

Raucous laughter floated to her left. She recognized her friends' voices. It sounded as if they were having a party! She darted around large hedges and found herself in a clearing.

Her friends were all sitting at a long table—plates, teacups, confetti, balloons, and party gear piled high atop the fringed purple tablecloth. A giant cake with pale green frosting tilted precariously in the center.

"Twinkle, twinkle little cat," Lyra sang from her seat at the head of the table, fake cat ears on her baseball cap. Teacups and saucers clattered as the group turned around to stare.

Adriane gaped, openmouthed.

"How I wonder where you're at."

"Who are you?" Adriane ran a hand over the table. It felt real enough.

"That's the mad catter, silly," Ozzie said, floating in an orange and blue porcelain teapot.

"Who are you supposed to be?" Adriane asked Ariel. The owl perched on the table, wearing a sea captain's hat.

"The mad hooter, of course," Ozzie said.

Drake held a dainty teacup in his huge paws, trying unsuccessfully to drink.

"What is going on here?" Adriane asked, dumbfounded.

"What is going on here?" Ozzie demanded, scrolling over a long sheet of paper that fell to the ground in waves. "You are down for two!"

Zach stood up, straightening his finely tailored pinstriped suit and wide red silk tie. "Everyone is supposed to bring a guest," he announced. "You can't come here all by yourself."

"Shhhhh!" Emily, her hair a mass of wild red ringlets, turned wide eyes to the boy. "She's always alone, she doesn't have anybody."

"Where is your hat?" Kara demanded. Her

170

golden hair was pulled into pigtails with two giant pink velvet bows that matched her frilly, doll-like dress. "You can't just come to our party looking like that."

"Listen to me!" Adriane exclaimed.

"I'm all ears." With a dramatic bow, Zach swept the cat ears off his head.

Adriane reached for the dragon's warm magic. "Drake, what's going on?"

"Tea party!" Drake snorted a burst of fire over his cup, making it boil.

This wasn't the spirit world, Adriane realized. She had fallen into the dream state. It shouldn't surprise me, she thought dully.

"I have to find Dreamer," she said, backing away from the bizarre scene.

"Who?"

Everyone looked at one another, confused.

"He's not on the list," Ozzie announced, cramming the scroll in the spout of the teapot.

"Dreamer!" Adriane cried. "My pack mate."

"Mistwolf?" Tweek leaped up and pirouetted across several muffins. "Don't be ridiculous. No one's seen one of those in years."

"They died out long ago," Emily added. "Thanks to you."

"What?" Adriane backed away in horror. "Don't even say that."

"That puppy was so cute!" Kara squealed.

"Where is he?" the warrior demanded.

"How should we know?" Zach asked. "You're the one who lost him."

"This is crazy," Adriane muttered. Things were getting hazy, her head was swimming. She had to get out of here, figure out what to do.

She ran to a path on the opposite side of the clearing, dodging between bushy branches laden with pastel marshmallows. She sped around a triangular hedge and stopped dead.

"It's her again!" Lyra exclaimed. A huge cowboy hat was crammed on her head.

Adriane's pulse pounded. "How did I get back here?"

"I know, I know!" Emily raised her hand in the air excitedly. The rainbow feathers sprouting from her wide-brimmed green hat swayed. "Every path leads here."

"Twingo!" Tweek, a mossy fedora on his head, twirled across the table.

Adriane stood staring.

"You can't do anything right." Kara adjusted her pink beret, giving Adriane a scornful look. "You are such a loser."

Adriane flopped into a large armchair at one end of the table. Orenda was dead, Dreamer lost, the magic of Ravenswood gone. Some earth warrior she was. She shook her head. This was surreal. She couldn't think clearly.

Suddenly, she gasped. "Where are your jewels?"

"What jewels?" Emily asked, looking over her sparkly plastic rings.

"Like this." Adriane held up her wrist—and stopped cold. Her wolf stone had vanished. Even her bracelet's tan line had disappeared completely. As if she'd never had it at all.

"I . . . I have to go," she whispered.

"Where?" Kara asked.

"How?" Emily asked.

"When?" Ozzie and Zach chorused.

"Hooo?" the mad hooter asked.

"I can world walk away from here right now." Adriane sprang to her feet. "Just watch me!"

She stepped forward, concentrating, and walked right into the table.

Everyone clapped.

"There's no place to go—you might as well stay here." Zach smiled.

"Nothing to do but eat cake." Ozzie dove into the green frosting.

"Just sit down and try to be normal like the rest of us," Kara said haughtily.

Somewhere inside, Adriane knew this was all wrong, but she just couldn't focus. Besides, they were right.

She slumped back down. She could walk away, but she could never leave—just keep going round and round, always ending up where she started. Destined to repeat everything again and again, all her mistakes, all her failures.

She might as well just give up. Move to Woodstock and paint fruit. There was nothing at Ravenswood for her now. She was never meant to have magic, or friends, or a real home. Why had she ever thought she didn't have to be alone?

She hung her head and closed her eyes, cutting off the jabbering noise of the party. This was just a dream. She wasn't alone. There had to be someone who could help her.

"Hey!" a familiar voice called out. "What's happening, dudes, and how come I wasn't invited?"

Adriane opened her eyes. A second Kara walked into the clearing, surveying the rainbow garden.

"Soooo . . . slacking off, are we?"

Oh, this is just great! Adriane thought. Of all the friends, I gotta pull in her!

"Who are you?" the catter called out, now wearing a thick wool hat with the earflaps pulled down.

"The question is . . ." The blazing star inspected the scene. "Who are *you?*"

"We know who we are." Lyra looked around. *"Don't we?"*

"What are you doing here?" The second Kara walked to Adriane's overstuffed chair. "Get up."

"Leave me alone." The warrior was suddenly exhausted.

"Say," the first Kara said, sizing up Kara Two. "You look very familiar."

Kara Two smiled. "You're quite beautiful."

"So true." Kara One giggled, pigtails swinging. "I wish I had hair like yours. Oh, I do!"

"But your fashion sense is, like, last Halloween."

"Oh, you wish you had these shoes!" Kara One wiggled her pointy green elf shoes.

"Yeah." Kara Two chuckled. "Next time I visit Saturn."

"Well, I have everything you have, and more." Kara One crossed her arms and pouted.

Kara Two tapped her chin thoughtfully. "Except for one teeny, tiny, eentsy, beensy, little thingy."

"What?"

"You're not real." Kara Two swung her glittering unicorn jewel.

"Get out!"

"She just got here," Ozzie complained, adjusting his giant polka-dot sombrero.

"Do they ever shut up on your planet?" With a brilliant flash of unicorn magic, the entire party freeze-framed. "Now, let's go!" Kara ordered Adriane.

The warrior yawned, eyes barely able to stay open. "It doesn't matter—I'll just end up here again."

"You have to find the power crystal."

"How'd you get in my dream, anyway?" Adriane asked.

"I have some experience in the astral planes."

Kara swirled her sparkling jewel in her fingers. "Not to mention this little power booster thing I like to call my network of friends. Came in quite handy in the Fairy Realms."

"Yeah, yeah, you saved everyone. Good for you."

Kara placed her hands on her hips. "So, you just going to sit here and sulk and leave the heavy lifting to your buds, or what?"

"I can't do anything."

"Adriane, this isn't real! We all need you."

The warrior eyed her suspiciously. Since when did the perfect blazing star need Adriane?

"This is only the dream state," Kara insisted. "You have to go all the way to the spirit world."

"It's too late." Adriane hung her head.

"Listen to me." Kara knelt in front of Adriane, taking the warrior's hands in hers. "Dawnrunner is okay."

Adriane looked up sharply. "Dawnrunner."

Kara nodded. "She was knocked around, but Emily helped her."

"Dreamer." Adriane's eyes widened.

Kara nodded. "If you don't go now, he and the rest of the mistwolves won't be so lucky. And we are going to lose Ravenswood."

"I don't even have my jewel."

"You mean that jewel?" Kara pointed at Adriane's wrist.

A small pinpoint of light shimmered. Adriane

squinted, looking harder, and the golden glow flashed brighter. The wolf stone appeared like magic.

"Now, come back to your real friends," Kara urged, releasing a sparkle of magic. It floated gently around the wolf stone, making it glow brightly.

Adriane felt the gentle touch of the healing stone, the strength of the dragon stone, the warm, fuzzy ferret stone, and the steadfast love of the animals. Her friends were all there, sending her their magic.

"Adriane, there isn't much time." Kara stood, gently pulling the warrior to her feet.

Adriane's heart thudded. Maybe it wasn't too late. Looking at Kara—the real Kara—Adriane knew her friend was telling the truth.

"Your dream is a total fashion disaster, anyway," the blazing star quipped. She held up her unicorn jewel, sending glittering magic sweeping over her and Adriane. "You ready?"

Adriane took a deep breath, held up her gem, and nodded.

Kara and Adriane faced each other and began to vanish.

"Hey, Barbie."

"Yeah, Xena?"

"Thanks."

In a flash of shining light, Adriane stepped into the spirit world.

She stood on cliffs of silver. A wide chasm gaped below her, seething with brilliant strands of wild magic.

A banshee whine wailed over the chasm. Like a whirling dervish, the ghostly demon spun, sending magic storms coursing through the air.

Adriane moved toward the edge of the cliff. "Storm," she called out.

The wolf's fragile connection with the crumbling spirit trail was fading fast. Wild magic swirled, picking away strands of mist. Storm was barely there.

Wolf stone blazing, Adriane sent the magic of her friends to Storm, praying she could hold the mist together.

The demon cackled, its mocking laughter echoing through the void. "The more magic the better," it sneered, voice raspy and unfamiliar.

That was not Orenda. It could only be the Spider Witch.

"Give me back my wolves!" Adriane ordered.

She jumped back as the glittering spirit trail shuddered beneath her feet, buckling in on itself. Without a pack mate to balance her, there was no way she could fight the witch. But Storm's and Dreamer's lives depended on her.

The wolf stone flashed wildly. Magic was seething inside of her, struggling to break free.

"The path to magic is not always through your friends," the witch said softly. "Free the wolf inside."

Adriane's blood boiled. But she was terrified to let

go. Would she be consumed by the savage beast, like Chain? Would she lose herself forever if she gave in?

Suddenly the air shifted as bands of magic tore apart. Something flew above the demon, flashing in and out of light and shadow—a multifaceted jewel.

The power crystal!

With a terrifying howl, the demon lunged, blackened hands swiping at the crystal. Using all the magic of Ravenswood, the demon reached toward the glittering prize, drawing it closer.

Adriane focused on the awesome crystal and raised her wolf stone. But a black blur flew through the air, knocking her aside.

Dreamer growled viciously, his emerald eyes completely veiled by burning bloodred fire. Pain lanced through her as Chain twisted inside Dreamer, devouring the pup's magic.

"Let him go, Chain!" the warrior commanded.

"You cannot save him, warrior." The black wolf's proud face stretched into a ghastly grin. *"You never could."*

Trapped beneath Chain's overbearing presence, Dreamer struggled to reach his pack mate. Adriane raised her wolf stone, mustering healing power and sending it to help Dreamer. She held out her other hand and fired a second beam of magic—to keep Storm alive.

"You cannot match our strength, warrior." The witch laughed.

Adriane's eyes widened as she realized what the witch was saying. "*You* are bonded to Chain?"

"Bonded?" the witch cackled. "Chain is *my* paladin!"

Dreamer suddenly lunged for the crystal, jaws opened wide. Adriane instinctively aimed her stone to stop him.

"Go ahead," the witch ordered, eyes blazing. "Do it!"

Dreamer's eyes flashed emerald as he tried to fight Chain's grip, but the ghost wolf was too strong.

Adriane screamed—her magic stretched beyond the breaking point.

"You must save the crystal of Avalon," Storm called, her mist wavering. *"Or the mistwolves will be lost."*

Wisps of glittering white pulled weakly around the warrior's magic. Her first pack mate was nearly gone.

What was she going to do? She couldn't help Dreamer without letting go of Storm. But without her magic, Storm would be lost forever.

She looked at the wolves, her heart ripping in two. She could only save one. No matter what she did, she was going to betray one of her pack mates.

Chapter 15

The Dark Sorceress drew in the pure magic of Avalon and breathed deeply, as if tasting its power for the first time. Overwhelmed with the rush, she barely noticed the black wolf that had materialized in the murky chamber, the dazzling power crystal in his jaws.

The Spider Witch saw him, though. "Give it to me," she commanded eagerly.

Eyes glinting blue and green, Chain wore Dreamer's face like a mask. The wolf advanced and carefully dropped the large gem in the witch's outstretched hand.

"Ravenswood is mine!" she cried, holding the prize high above her head. The magic of Avalon cast gleaming halos onto the lair's rough stone walls.

Across the chamber, the sorceress's animal eyes gleamed. Silver hair blew back from her face as the magic washed over her, reawakening her power. Yet there was something not quite right.

The crystal had been tainted by the touch of an animal.

"I suggest you examine the crystal a little more closely," she said, retreating from the cascading light.

The witch's eyes sparked with anger. The crystal was vibrating, rattling in her hands. Concentrating, she held the jewel tightly as tendrils of glittering mist shimmered around the faceted edges.

Suddenly the crystal began to rock furiously as a low hum emanated from its sparkling center. The noise got louder, until it crescendoed into a chorus of terrifying howls.

The witch turned to the black wolf. "What's happened to it?"

With a golden flash, the mist pulled together.

A dark-haired girl stood in the chamber, her dark eyes burning. Upon her wrist, the wolf stone pulsed dangerously.

Adriane looked around. "What a dump."

Surprised by the girl's sudden appearance, the Spider Witch stepped back, tightening her grip on the shuddering power crystal. "You can't possibly think you can walk in here and take the crystal."

The warrior advanced, her wolf stone blazing like a sun. "I brought a few friends."

Adriane whirled, slamming rings of golden fire into the witch. The crystal flew out of the evil witch's clutches. In a flash, it vanished as glittering streams of misty light coursed through the chamber. The magical mist assumed ghostly forms as the spirit pack poured out. Hundreds of wolves sparkling black, blue, silver, red, gold, and white filled the chamber.

"The spirit pack!" Chain's voice echoed from Dreamer as the wolf snarled, furiously yapping and biting at the air.

The Dark Sorceress watched intently. So, the spirit pack had been trapped inside the power crystal. A hidden smile twisted her lips. Her theories had been correct all along. She had used the mistwolves before to lure the magic of Avalon. There was no doubt now that *their* magic was connected to the very source of all magic.

"Chain, kill the wolf!" the Spider Witch shrieked.

"I don't think so," Adriane said coolly.

Hundreds of wolves descended on Dreamer, howling as they enveloped him in ghostly blue light. Adriane could feel the Spider Witch's spell twisting at Chain. She understood now: The wolf was not the witch's true paladin, but a prisoner. Just like Orenda.

Chain's anguished howl tore through the chamber as his glowing form separated from Dreamer and was pulled into the swirling wolf storm. With a last yelp, Dreamer was free.

"Your spell has been broken," the voices of the ancient wolves snarled.

With a loud rip, the top corner of the Ravenswood tapestry fell, strands of webbing unraveling.

The witch bolted toward the weaving. Her robe fluttered, then fell to the floor.

Adriane was stunned.

The Spider Witch's head and torso had warped into a swollen spider abdomen from which eight thick spider legs protruded. The faceted yellow eyes of an insect had monstrously distorted her face. Hair writhing like it was alive, the Spider Witch climbed up the tapestry, frantically trying to re-weave it. More spiders emerged, crawling over her heavy legs.

The spirit pack, now thousands strong, swirled in the room, a maelstrom of wolf power.

Wisps of Ravenswood's tangled magic disintegrated into smoke as the witch's spell broke apart. Adriane caught the remnants of the demon fluttering in the air before it vanished.

"No!" The witch staggered. The weaving unraveled, sending her tumbling to the floor.

With a booming crash, the ceiling crumbled to smoking rubble, leaving a gaping hole. Through it, the spirit pack swirled upward, streaming into the dark sky overhead.

Adriane and the witch saw the floating crystal at the same time. With a shrill cry, the Spider Witch lunged, clawing at it with all her might.

Adriane whipped golden fire through the air, ensnaring the crystal.

"Help me!" the witch cried frantically.

Adriane flicked her eyes to the shifting shadows.

"Impressive, warrior." The Dark Sorceress stood before her, eyes glowing with hunger. "The magic of the mistwolves is truly breathtaking."

"Choke on it," Adriane snarled, wolf stone flashing.

The sorceress raised her arms, trying to pull the spirit pack to her.

Dreamer at her side, Adriane wrapped a shield of wolf fire around the escaping pack.

The ghost wolves howled, disappearing into the night skies.

Red fire crackled from the power crystal as the Spider Witch lashed out.

Adriane staggered back, but kept her jewel trained on the pack. In that moment, the witch pulled the crystal into her hands. Clutching the prize, the Spider Witch scurried from the chamber.

"I see you have a new mistwolf," the Dark Sorceress sneered. "Used up the other one already, did we?"

"You will never take their magic!" Adriane cried, swinging the fire directly at the sorceress, pounding at her in a frenzy of strikes.

Palms held out, the sorceress did her best to deflect the blows. But she was not at full strength. She could not stand against the warrior and the power of the spirit pack.

"I want the crystal!" Adriane ordered, arms raised, black wolf crouched by her side.

"It's out of my hands, so to speak."

Adriane moved to the door but stopped short. A

huge shadow fell across the stone floor. An immense insect, oily wings shimmering upon its back, blocked the way. Like a giant beetle, black armor covered its torso. Green insect eyes gleamed as antennae twitched, sending out secret signals.

With a hiss, its black wings sprang open. Hundreds of spiders charged into the room, shrieking hungrily.

Wolf fire shot toward the creatures, slicing through thick abdomens and legs.

"Bug off!"

Adriane swung a circle of fire around her and Dreamer as more spiders spilled into the chamber.

Suddenly, the lair rumbled, shaking the very foundations of the castle. Adriane felt the magic of the power crystal tickling along her skin as if she were walking through spiderwebs.

"What is that witch doing with the crystal?" Adriane demanded.

"She's a spider," the sorceress said, smirking. "Think about it."

Adriane looked at the destroyed weaving, its strands now littering the floor.

"Too bad you won't be able to save your new wolf." The sorceress smiled, vampire teeth gleaming, eyes focused on the wolf stone. "There's no way out. Losing two wolves—that's got to hurt."

Adriane's heart pounded. It was like her nightmare come to life, but this time she was not going to fail her pack mate, either of them.

Adriane looked skyward to be sure the spirit pack had all escaped. She knew Storm was bravely leading them onto the spirit trail. Now, she had to flee this chamber of horrors and make her stand at Ravenswood, surrounded by her friends. But she had one thing to do first.

Following a slight gesture of Adriane's hand, Dreamer drew close to her side.

"Who did *you* lose?" She stared at the sorceress then gave her pack mate a nod. Dreamer went first, shimmering to mist and vanishing. "Think about it."

Adriane centered her elemental magic, feeling the bright power of the wolf stone wash over her. She had been afraid of the wolf within, but fear had blinded her. Standing on the cliffs of the spirit world, torn between Storm and Dreamer, she had looked into the heart of the power crystal and finally understood. The spirit pack touched every wolf, balancing raw power with ancient magic. Embracing the magical essence rather than the pure animal, Adriane had made her choice. She had released the wolf inside, diving into the power crystal itself.

In a flash, Adriane faded to mist and joined her pack mates.

Welcomed by the spirits of the mistwolves, Adriane

and Dreamer flew onto the glowing spirit trail. Wolf power, past, present, and future, surged through Adriane. It filled her entire being—the knowledge, experience, love, and strength that was at the very core of every mistwolf. This was her magic, too, as much as it was Dreamer's and Storm's.

"Run with us, wolf sister."

The voices of the wolves fell gently in her mind.

The spirit trail melted away. Mighty trees sprang up, surrounding them in lush greens, browns, and golds. The smell of the forests filled Adriane's senses.

"My heart soars to see you, warrior."

A silver wolf moved to her side, strong and full of magic. Stormbringer.

Adriane smiled at her pack mate.

Fiery reds, ocean blues, brilliant yellows, and deep forest greens curled and danced, flowing across the sky.

The pack came to the trail's end, where sand and sea met, where worlds joined. Their vision of the past shimmered before Adriane's eyes. Great crystalline towers rose, catching glints of light. Giant interlocking rocks set in an immense jigsaw puzzle led the way to the crystal city floating in an ocean of time. Creatures of untold beauty and power inhabited the city.

"What is this place?" Adriane asked, awestruck.

"Avalon," the wolves said.

"As it was."

"As it will be again."

The vision splintered, replaced with a dark, mist-shrouded island.

"What happened?" Adriane asked.

"Avalon was destroyed."

The spirit pack swirled around her, many wolves speaking in one voice.

"The magical creatures fled to Aldenmor. Mistwolves lost touch with the spirit trail, reverting to savagery. Pack leaders came to believe bonding with humans was harmful."

"What happened to Chain?" Adriane asked.

"The wizard Gardener was trying to rebuild Avalon. He won the trust of the wolf, Chain—but they were not meant to bond."

Adriane listened intently.

"The path to Avalon can only be found by humans and magical animals working together, even though there are those that will try otherwise. Gardener fought the Spider Witch. As she fell into the Otherworlds, she bound Chain to her. Gardener could not protect his pack mate."

Adriane nodded. Stormbringer pressed close to her side.

"Chain sent a clear message to the pack: Humans do not belong with mistwolves."

"So Moonshadow took the pack into hiding, afraid humans would destroy them all."

Several ghost wolves faced Adriane and Storm, silver eyes shining. *"Your bond with Storm changed the course of the spirit trail forever. You have taken the first step to restoring Avalon."*

Adriane reached out in wonder, her wolf stone flaring as her magic touched the magnificent spirits. "Not all humans betray their pack mates."

"Take from the past and lead us into the future, warrior."

A bright beacon blinked in the distance.

"The pack calls you."

"We must go to them."

"May you always run free."

Adriane burst into the glade in a blaze of golden light. To one side, Dreamer stood, his midnight-black fur gleaming. On her other side stood the great silver mistwolf Stormbringer, her golden eyes shining as the wolf saw the friends she had left behind months ago.

"Storm!"

"Dreamer!"

The mages, animals, and mistwolves rushed forward as Adriane threw her arms around both pack mates, happy tears falling down her cheeks. She hadn't thought she would ever feel Storm's solid, reassuring presence again. And now she was really here, standing in the forests of Ravenswood, where she belonged—alive!

"I don't believe it!" Emily cried as she and Kara hugged Storm.

"Welcome back!" Ozzie beamed, shoving in to hug Storm's chest.

"Woohoot!" Ariel tooted, swirling around the wolf as Lyra nosed in to greet her friend.

"It is good to see everyone again," Storm said, lips turned up at the corners in a wolfish grin.

"You honor us." Moonshadow bowed before Storm. *"The spirit pack runs strong."*

"The magic of Avalon flows through us all." Dawn-runner came up beside Adriane, sky blue eyes shining brilliantly.

Adriane hugged the alpha female as the wolf nuzzled her cheek. The entire pack surrounded her, everyone eager to welcome back Storm and Dreamer.

"You have grown strong," Stormbringer said to Dreamer, nudging his nose with her own.

"Pack mates grow strong together," Dreamer said.

Adriane looked at both of her pack mates, old and new. "Storm, I—"

"The pack takes care of its own," the silver wolf said, rubbing against Dreamer in a sign of affection.

The warrior smiled, relieved.

Colored bubbles suddenly burst in the air above them.

"Look!" Ozzie jumped up and down, pointing. "Something's coming through!"

Splat! Splooie! Sparf! Sploof! Sploot!

Five worried mini dragons plummeted from the sky, falling on the mages.

"Kaaraa!" Goldie squeaked, hugging the blazing star's neck with her bright yellow wings.

Purple Barney peeled himself off Zach's shoulder and stood nose to nose with Drake. "Ooo."

Red Fiona whizzed happily around Emily, nearly colliding with orange Blaze, who barreled straight into Ozzie.

"Hi, Fred!" Adriane hugged the blue dragonfly that landed on her shoulder.

"Finally!" Goldie scowled at Kara.

"How do you expect me to do anything without my favorite mini?" Kara scratched her little friend between her golden wings. "I missed you, too."

"Adriane, you did it!" Emily smiled, arms draped around Storm.

"You saved them all," Zach exclaimed. "Dreamer, Storm, the spirit pack, the wolves of Aldenmor—all the mistwolves!"

"And Ravenswood is totally web free, too," Kara pronounced, unicorn jewel glittering.

Drake nosed Adriane, puffing proudly, as the d'flies circled her head squealing and chirping.

"Aaaaggg." Tweek suddenly tottered past, leaning on a mossy rock as twigs dropped from his torso.

"Now what?" Kara demanded. "Possessed by the Ghost of Christmas Past?"

Adriane scanned the forests nervously.

Moonshadow and Dawnrunner sniffed at the air.

"Something is different here," Dreamer said.

"What's wrong?" Emily asked, suddenly sensing danger.

"The spirit pack was trapped in the power crystal." Adriane blinked as her wolf stone sputtered on her wrist, the bright light burning her eyes. "I freed them, but the witch got the crystal."

"She is using our magic against us," Moonshadow snarled.

"That's ridicu—Gah!" Ozzie's jewel sparked, sending him flying backward.

"Ozzie!" Emily ran her healing stone over the ferret, but the gem crackled in a shower of sparks.

The mistwolves growled, scanning the forest.

"What's happening?" Zach asked, blue eyes wide as his dragon stone pulsed erratically.

With a subtle flick of her wrist, Dreamer and Storm flanked Adriane, standing strong on either side. The warrior reached with her wolf senses, gently touching the forest. The trees lived, but there was no magic flowing through their roots.

"Can't you feel it?" she asked.

"I don't feel—anything," Kara gasped.

"It's gone!" Emily cried.

The warrior nodded grimly. "Orenda is dead."

"No sylph, no magic," Tweek wheezed.

The mages looked at one another, the horrible realization sinking in: The magic of Ravenswood was gone.

Chapter 16

Lightning crackled atop the Rocking Stone as droplets of dark, oily rain began to fall.

Emily tried to send healing magic into the gathering puddles of dark magic, but her gem sparked and fizzled. "What's wrong with our jewels?"

"Your jewels are tied to Ravenswood," Tweek answered. "Theoretically"—Tweek stuck loose twigs back into his mass—"if the witch controls Ravenswood, she could control your jewels as well."

Dank droplets fell, drenching the trees and seeping into the forest floor.

"It's spreading fast," Dawnrunner said, her golden white coat streaked with black rain.

Adriane and the spirit pack had destroyed the Ravenswood tapestry and broken the spell, but it had served its purpose, creating a demon to attract the power crystal. Now the Spider Witch was going to complete the rest of her plan.

"She's using the power crystal to weave her own magic into Ravenswood," Adriane exclaimed.

"Our friends in the Fairy Realms said she's going

to try to re-weave the entire magic web!" Kara said, remembering what the Goblin Prince had told her about the Spider Witch's plan.

"She been after the preserve all along," Zach realized. "If her plan is to re-weave the web, she's starting with Ravenswood."

The rain fell harder, darkening the sky as if night had fallen. Everything felt completely unbalanced as the magic seeped deeper, lulling the forest into a dark dream.

"What are we supposed to do?" Kara asked.

Adriane frantically wiped oily rain from her arms and legs. She hadn't come this far to lose it all now.

Suddenly Dreamer stood tall, eyes flashing as he raised his nose in the air.

"Pack mate."

"What you got?"

"Magic."

"Show me."

The black mistwolf sniffed the ground and trotted to a sheltered hollow. Storm ran after him, using her magic to protect him from the toxic rain.

Lightning flashed, illuminating the trees in ghostly light.

The group gathered around Dreamer as he started to dig through a pile of charred twigs. Adriane felt the magic burn him as he nosed aside slabs of shriveled bark.

Suddenly Dreamer stood back.

There, poking through the sodden ashes, was a lone flower—a puffy dandelion sparkling with bright colors, like a sphere of tiny magic gems.

Emily ran over for a closer look. "It's a rainbow flower!" the healer gasped. "Phelonius spread these all over the preserve last summer."

"A phelower!" Kara exclaimed.

Phelonius was the first fairy creature the girls had ever met. He had appeared when Adriane and Emily had discovered their jewels. Along with Ozzie, the mages helped the giant bear-like creature get home to Aldenmor. They'd heard nothing from him since.

"LOooOkie!" The five dragonflies swarmed around the bright bloom, scattering the puffy seeds in a poof of activity. The ground shimmered. Clear, pristine puddles remained where the twinkling bits had fallen.

Adriane's wolf stone flashed bright gold. "Yes!"

"Here it is." Tweek held up his HORARFF, projecting an image of the rainbow flower. "*Flora rainbowpufficus* produces large quantities of raw magic, which can be harvested in a variety of ways. They are elemental in nature."

"If we can get the seeds to grow and bloom, we can replace the magic of Ravenswood!" Adriane exclaimed.

"Easier said than done," Tweek sighed, leaning against Storm. "There's something I'm just not seeing, if I could just put my twig on it—"

"What do we need, a Miracle-Gro spell?" Kara asked.

Tweek's quartz eyes practically bulged out of his grassy head. "Twingo!"

The little E. F. took off, scurrying back through the glade to the Rocking Stone.

Everyone raced after him.

Tweek studied the glowing symbols on the tower's base. "Of course!"

"What?" Ozzie demanded.

The E. F. grabbed Ozzie, pressing his nose to the stone. "Look!"

"Gah!"

"These symbols. It's not a message—they're directions!"

"You mean this is a recipe for growing rainbow flowers?" Ozzie guessed.

"Precisely!" Tweek pointed a twig at a flower-shaped symbol.

"So that's what Phel was doing," Emily exclaimed. "Making sure we'd always have magic in Ravenswood."

"Let's go for it!" Kara called out.

"Inconceivable!" Tweek faced the mages. "Each one of you must add elemental magic needed to make the pufficus."

"Hurryupicus!" Ozzie shook Tweek.

"Earth can't thrive without water, air, fire, or time," Tweek explained. "Each element must work together in harmony, strengthening all the others. Only together do you have the power to save Ravenswood."

"We can do this," Adriane declared. "We have to!"

The warrior led her friends back to the glade. Everything they had learned about magic would be put to the test.

"Everyone team up with your magical animals and form a circle," Tweek shouted, racing after the group.

The mages and animals ringed the seedlings twinkling upon the forest floor. The five dragonflies flew about excitedly, each landing on a mage's shoulder.

The E. F. nodded, looking the group over. "Zach and Drake are a powerful time combination, Kara has Lyra and her paladin for fire, Adriane has the mistwolves for earth, and you two—"

Emily and Ozzie stood in the circle with only Fiona and Blaze.

The two d'flies looked at each other and zipped over to Kara.

"Fine!" Ozzie called out.

Ariel fluttered over the group, landing on Emily's arm.

"Thank you," Emily said, nuzzling the white owl.

"We'll all help Emily and Ozzie," Kara instructed, unicorn jewel sparkling with diamond light.

Tweek waved his twigs at the mages. "But you still have to figure out how to work together."

"I know, spellsinging!" Kara said, twirling her unicorn jewel confidently.

The mages had learned music was a powerful way to combine their magic.

"A spellsong could harmonize your different types of magic," Tweek agreed.

Adriane nodded. "It's time we did a little magic weaving of our own."

"Me, me, me, me," Goldie sang.

"You, you, you," Fred sang back.

Wolf stone glowing, Adriane stepped toward Emily, Kara, Zach, and Ozzie. The mages joined hands and paws, jewels sparkling with intertwining magic. With a rousing cheer, they broke apart and walked to their animal friends, jewels raised and ready.

Tweek looked to Emily. "First up, we need water."

"We're on it." Emily stepped to the center of the circle, Ariel perched on her arm.

The animals of Ravenswood gathered with the mistwolves and Drake ready to send the healer magic.

"Go, Emily!" the animals cheered.

Emily closed her eyes in concentration. Then she started to sway, arms moving in a dance.

Shimmering, showering
Droplets like jewels
Fountain of sky
Awake, and renew

Emily sang, spinning in a circle, her long red hair flying around her. Fiona, Blaze, Goldie, Barney, and Fred sparkled in the air as they danced with Ariel. The lake bubbled and churned, shooting arcs of water in rhythm with Emily's soaring spellsong.

Petals of green and blue blossomed from the rainbow stone, sinking into the black clouds overhead. Everyone in the circle gave magic to the healer, as streaks of purple and turquoise raced through the clouds.

Turning and turning
This circle of friends
One world, one home
Begins where it ends

Glittering rain fell, diamond white and pure as a spring shower.

"Wonderful!" Adriane swayed to Emily's song, feeling the seedlings springing to life as they drank in the sweet, clean water.

Cheers rang across the glade as Emily, the d'flies, and Ariel took a bow.

"The seedlings need the heat of fire to bloom," Tweek instructed.

"Sun team!" Kara and Goldie shimmied into the center of the circle with Lyra. The blazing star shut her eyes, concentrated, and called upon the magic of fire. "Starfire, I need you." The unicorn jewel flared with bright firemental magic. "We all need you."

In a meteoric *whoosh*, a bolt of fire streaked across the sky. Iridescent orange-and-red flames twisted together and formed a magnificent stallion with strong muscles and flowing mane and tail.

Everyone gaped in awe at the amazing creature that stood before them.

"Blazing star." The firemental stallion bent his head over Kara's shoulder as she hugged him, unicorn jewel instantly covering her in a protective shield.

"You came for me," she said, barely holding back tears of joy.

"I am for you."

With a swift leap, Kara swung up onto his back. The incredible stallion reared up on his hind legs, flames licking the air.

Lyra and Goldie flapped their golden wings and hovered on either side of the blazing rider.

Kara hugged Starfire's flaming neck. "Let's rock!"

Gleaming, streaming
Star shining bright
Color the land
With your blanket of light

Prisms of light streamed from the unicorn jewel, forming a bright rainbow. The fire stallion's hooves burned brightly as he raced into the air, pulling the rainbow after him in a curving arc.

Goldie and Lyra followed Starfire, looping and weaving around the growing rainbow.

As the sun team reached the top of the rainbow, the clouds parted. Bright sunlight spilled over the forest like a golden curtain. Small seedlings burst through the soil, dazzling bright points of color in the grass.

"Excellent!" Adriane said, sensing the flowers reaching for the firemental magic.

Everyone cheered as Starfire landed, Kara's arms held high. The rainbow stretched across the brilliant blue sky.

Tweek nodded. "The flowers need time to grow and bloom."

"I am the germinator!" Zach exclaimed, stepping into the circle as Drake stomped forward, Barney on his head.

The boy held his dragon stone high in the air. Drake threw back his head and roared, sending a burst of flame into the sky. Red waves of magic swirled from Zach's jewel, rippling over the seedlings.

Hours to days
Morning to night
Everything blooms
In its own perfect time

Rainbow flowers popped up like popcorn, blooming and spreading as Zach's dragon magic fast-forwarded the flowers' growing cycle. Sparkling puffs blossomed everywhere until there were hundreds shining across the floor of the glade.

Adriane felt the flowers, heavy with magic, swaying on their stems. "Okay, they're ready." She hugged Drake's neck and high-fived Zach.

"We need wind to scatter the seeds," Tweek directed.

A flock of baby quiffles shoved Ozzie forward.

"Go, Ozzie!"

Ozzie closed his eyes tight, ferret stone glowing bright orange. Slowly he started floating up from the ground, until he was nose to nose with Starfire.

Ozzie opened his eyes. "What are you looking at?"

The stallion looked down.

"Gah!"

The ferret plummeted to the ground. Quickly springing to his feet, he adjusted his ferret stone and tried again.

Wings all a-flutter
Trees bend and sway
The whistle of wind
Brings new life today

A gentle breeze ruffled the quiffles' head feathers as the d'flies fluttered over Ozzie's head.

"We need more," Adriane called out, sensing the magic coming loose from the flowers. "Come on, Air Team. You're almost there!"

The mages and animals directed all their magic toward the ferret stone.

Ozzie's fur sparked and frizzled as the breeze increased. He bore down harder, sending a stiff wind sweeping across the grass. The rainbow seeds came loose and floated through the air in a twinkling cloud.

"I think I'm getting the hang of this!" Ozzie exulted.

"Fuzzy rocks!" a quiffle cheered.

"HelP!" Ozzie's stone glowed as a huge gust of wind ripped through the preserve, sweeping him off his feet and tumbling him into the trees.

"Excellent!" Tweek approved, then turned to Adriane. "The last step is weaving the magic into the earth."

Adriane hugged Fred as the mistwolves moved in around her. With a nod, the warrior stepped forward. "We're ready."

She could feel the melody building in the heart of her powers, her senses tingling with the magic floating across the glade.

"It's the Dreamer team!"

The pack gathered around the warrior, sending her the power of their renewed magic. Storm stood at her right side, Dreamer to her left, balancing the wave of glowing golden wolf light spreading out from her jewel.

The wolves howled softly, a low whine that rose and fell in pitch. Moving to the earth beat, the sound became a song—the song of Orenda.

Rhythm of life
Spirit of song
Growing together
Our hearts beat as one

Thunder rumbled and Dreamer cocked his ears, listening to the mighty growls. Adriane closed her eyes, letting the magic rush through her as the spirit pack, thousands strong, swept across the sky.

Releasing her inner wolf, she joined her pack mates.

Warrior and wolves shimmered and vanished. A cloud of glowing mist hovered where they had stood a second before.

Suddenly Adriane was everywhere at once. The mistwolves swept over the entire preserve, seeking the magic that floated in the air. Adriane held on tight, her essence interwoven with the pack. They were united in a single consciousness, with one purpose: to save the forest. Clear and focused, she sank down into the earth, pulling the magic with her.

Turning and turning
This circle of friends
One world, one home
Begins where it ends

Adriane weaved the magic deep into the earth. A pulsing rhythm pounded in time with her heart, enveloping her with the full power of the earth symphony. Every tiny flower, every creature, every tree was a crucial part of the song. But none of it would flourish unless all living things were in balance, supporting one another in harmony—like her circle of friends.

Deeper she went, treasuring the miracle of life at the very core of earth magic. With Storm and Dreamer by her side, a sphere of swirling light enveloping them all, Adriane wove mist back to solid form.

In the middle of the light stood a sylph, her flowing, fairy form surrounded by flowering vines. She greeted Adriane and the wolves with a radiant smile. The angelic beauty of her delicate features contrasted sharply with the craggy roots that spread from her arms and legs.

"Remember this song," the ancient creature said, her voice resonant with the power of the earth.

Adriane listened in wonder.

"It is who you are."

The melody floated through her senses. The

sylph's song held the essence of every living thing in Ravenswood, from the oaks bordering Wolf Run Pass, to the rivers rolling through the deep ravines, to the wide, grassy expanse of the portal field.

In the soaring notes, Adriane heard the echoes of wolf howls. Each refrain flowed into the next, telling of a vast network of forests woven together, of worlds connected.

Adriane felt her pack mates at her side and understood.

"I am alone but also part of the pack, many wolves with one voice."

The fairy creature nodded, sudden sadness washing over her deep eyes. The melody wavered, notes falling flat.

"What's wrong?" Adriane asked.

"Without a forest spirit, the magic will not last."

Adriane faltered. Without Orenda, the magic of the rainbow flowers could not sustain Ravenswood. The final piece was still missing.

"I am ready." Storm stepped forward, head held high.

The sylph regarded Adriane, eyes full of compassion. "The mistwolf is a part of us."

"Storm?" Adriane's heart wrenched as she realized what her pack mate was about to do.

"This has always been my path, warrior," Storm said, her warm golden eyes full of love.

Adriane knelt nose to nose with the silver wolf. "But I just got you back," she whispered, fighting back tears.

"And now I am going home."

"Home." Adriane smiled, finally realizing the truth.

Dreamer bowed low. *"I will keep her safe."*

"So will I."

Adriane hugged Storm, holding on tight. She would remember this moment forever. "I love you, Storm."

"I am with you, Adriane," Storm said to her pack mate. *"Now and forever."*

The sylph reached out. Stormbringer walked to her, silver fur dissolving to starlight. Adriane gazed into her bonded's golden eyes. Then, the wolf vanished.

The mist shone in the center of the glade, separating and transforming back to warrior and wolf. The rest of the pack stood around Adriane and Dreamer, howling joyfully.

"You did it!" Zach cried, hugging her as Drake danced from foot to foot.

A huge cheer erupted. Her friends gathered around, laughing, hugging, and crying.

Around them, the forest spread out majestically, trees and grass shimmering with vibrant greens and browns. A gentle breeze ruffled the sun-bright leaves. Magic flooded through the preserve, clean and pure.

Ravenswood stood stronger than ever.

Emily looked around, concerned. "Where's Storm?"

"She's right here." Adriane smiled, wolf stone glowing bright silver. "Home."

Chapter 17

"It's a symphony," Adriane said.

"How so?" her father, Luc, asked, clearly pleased.

Emily, Kara, Adriane, and Zach marveled over a series of swooping stainless-steel circles and squares, playing with the light like a mirror.

"Different elements working together to make something beautiful," Adriane responded.

They stood in a wide gallery lined with large, frosted windows. Luxuriant light played over the serene sculptures.

"I've never seen anything like it, Mr. Charday," Zach said.

"It's amazing," Emily added.

"Minimal but elegant." Kara's blue eyes were narrowed in concentration. "Very power style."

"They're awesome!" Adriane declared proudly as her dad slung his arm around her shoulder. "I'd love to see how you make these."

Luc smiled warmly. "We can work on them this summer . . . if you'd like."

"Sure, that would be great," she answered.

"Wonderful show."

Everyone turned at the sound of Gran's voice. Her bright purple dress swayed as she walked confidently across the gallery with Willow, her dark eyes full of renewed strength.

"She's wearing me out," Willow said. "You'd think it was me who just got out of the hospital yesterday."

"I haven't felt this good in years," Gran said, dark eyes dancing.

"I've been showing off the big story." Willow held up a copy of the *Stonehill Gazette*. "You guys are front page."

"WOLF COMES HOME!" was the headline atop a picture of Dreamer surrounded by kids from Stonehill Middle School.

"The school started a petition to keep Ravenswood open," Emily said.

"There're over one thousand names on it!" Kara added.

"They're even sending it out to other schools in the area," Adriane said excitedly. Tiff, Molly, Heather, Marcus, Joey, Kyle, and the gang had really pulled through.

"Dreamer's famous!" Gran read. "The official mascot of Ravenswood."

Luc shook his head. "To think he escaped the zoo and walked over a hundred miles to get back to the preserve."

"Wow!" Kara exclaimed. "Uh, I mean . . . poor little guy couldn't bear to be without us."

"Ravenswood is clearly where Dreamer belongs." Willow faced her daughter. "You've both made a good home there."

"Mrs. Windor doesn't seem like the kind of woman who gives up," Luc said thoughtfully.

Gran snorted. "Windor has no choice. She's been outvoted again, since Dreamer got such good publicity for the preserve."

Luc looked over at a well-dressed man waving to him.

"Willow, I want you to meet the museum director," Luc said, nodding to him.

"I'll be right there," Willow said as Luc walked away.

"Kara, let's show Zach the rest of the exhibits," Emily suggested.

"Cool." Kara and Emily slipped their arms into Zach's, pulling the boy into another room full of paintings.

Grandmother, mother, and daughter—three generations—regarded one another.

"Adriane, your grandmother and I have been talking," Willow said, breaking the silence.

"And we think it's best for you to stay where you are," Gran finished.

"Yes!"

"I've never seen you happier, and your friends love you very much," Willow said.

"Yeah, they're okay." Adriane smiled.

Willow clasped her daughter's hands. "Whatever this connection is that you have with Ravenswood, I think it's a good thing. It's almost as if you have an angel there, looking out for you. I just couldn't hear her."

"Maybe you just didn't listen," Adriane said.

"Maybe I couldn't understand what was being said." Willow took Adriane in her arms. "You are a wild spirit, baby girl. Don't ever let it be tamed."

Adriane closed her eyes, hugging her mother tightly.

❧　❧　❧

Sunset washed over the forest, kissing the trees with waves of red, orange, and purple. Adriane stood with the wolves near the lake in the glade. Moon-shadow lifted his head and howled, a long wail that echoed into the sky. Dawnrunner, Dreamer, and the other wolves joined in the chorus. They were welcoming the new spirit of Ravenswood.

Across the glade, her friends stood listening to the wolf song.

"How's it going?" The warrior stepped forward, the wolf stone upon her wrist shining luminous silver edged with gold—Storm's colors.

"Your jewel is amazing!" Tweek inspected her wrist. "Stormbringer is a powerful paladin."

Kara twirled her pink and white unicorn jewel and regarded the warrior. "You know, I think Adriane's jewel is really another color."

"What do you mean?" Adriane asked, anxiously studying her jewel.

"Every time she gets near Zach, she turns completely red."

"I do not!"

Zach walked up as the girls giggled. "The preserve looks great."

Adriane flushed red as a tomato.

"You can feel her here." He smiled at Adriane, gesturing to the lush trees and sparkling lake.

"Zach, there's a big school dance coming up before summer break," Kara said slyly.

"I've never been to one of those," Zach exclaimed, looking at the warrior.

Adriane blushed again. "It's a date."

"All right!" The boy beamed.

"Oh me, me, me, me." Tweek twirled by, his HORARFF zipping through images. "We have a lot of work to do."

"Tweek, was Avalon really destroyed?" asked Emily.

"From what the spirit pack told Adriane, it would seem so."

"I saw the island," Kara said thoughtfully. "But it was all under mist."

"Even if Avalon was destroyed, the magic still runs

strong. And that means it can be rebuilt." Tweek regarded the mages as the animals of Ravenswood gathered around. "There are several ways to control the magic of Avalon, theoretically. The Dark Sorceress tried to control it through magical animals. The Spider Witch wants to re-weave the entire web. But the only sure way is by returning the nine crystals."

"Eight," Kara said sadly.

"Yes, one was destroyed. Two are with the Fairimentals. And now one is in the Spider Witch's hands."

"So what's next?" Adriane asked.

"We go after the other five," Ozzie said adamantly. "Then figure it out."

"We'll have to be ready." Tweek tottered back and forth. "We have two Level Ones"—he looked to Emily and Zach—"two Level Twos . . ."

Adriane and Kara smiled at each other, Dreamer and Lyra standing proudly by their sides.

"And something else entirely." Tweek looked at the ferret.

"Hey!" the ferret protested.

"Ozzie is very important. A clear case of elemental transformation."

"Transformation—now *that* is interesting," Ozzie said.

"Precisely. You think the Fairimentals just picked any elf to turn into a rodent?"

"Weasel," Kara said.

"Mammal," Emily added.

"Whatever!" Tweek hobbled about. "What I mean is, you have powerful magic, Ozzie."

Ozzie scratched his chin, pondering the revelation.

"The mistwolves will return to Aldenmor and protect the Fairimentals," Moonshadow said.

Adriane nodded, jewel sparking.

"You take care of Dreamer," Dawnrunner said.

Leaning down, Adriane rubbed her head against the wolf.

"Pup, you sure are a pawful of trouble!" Moonshadow growled at Dreamer.

"I learned from the best." Dreamer stood and stretched, his black fur glistening in the fading sun. He smiled the relaxed grin of a confident wolf, opening his mouth and letting his scarlet tongue loll out.

"Just wait until you have pups of your own," Adriane told Moonshadow.

"That time is coming soon." Dawnrunner's eyes twinkled as she snuffled in his ear.

Moonshadow's eyes opened wide.

Everyone cheered.

The pack leader leaped happily around his mate. Zach grabbed his wolf brother and pulled him down so that he half jumped, half fell into the grass.

"Let's get wigjiggy with it!" Ozzie shuffled and leaped, landing on his rump.

Emily and Kara danced with Ozzie, Zach, Drake, Lyra, and Ariel. The dragonflies zipped overhead, careening and twirling in joyous celebration.

Adriane hugged Dreamer, her wolf stone shining like moonlight. She let her pack mate join the joyous romp as she turned and walked across the glade.

Adriane had never felt like she belonged anywhere. Torn between different schools, between the wolf pack and her friends, she'd never fit in completely with any group. Storm had made her feel strong and connected to her magic. When Storm was lost, Adriane had lost herself, too.

Now Storm would be there for her, a paladin who would always come when Adriane needed her most. But Dreamer would be by her side every day, and she intended to make the most of it. They both had so much to learn about their magic. Her bond with Dreamer would never be like her bond with Storm, but that was how it should be. Dreamer was unique. He held a special place in her heart that was his alone.

She reached out to the forest and felt Storm's loving presence all around her.

The last of the day's pink glow filtered through the trees, reflecting off her jewel. A million facets of brilliant love turned in the silver light.

Since losing Storm, Adriane had kept her heart locked in a cage. Now, she was moving on. She had allowed the wolf in her to run free, and in doing so she had unlocked a part of herself. She didn't know what would happen or where she'd be tomorrow. But she was strong; she was fierce. She was a warrior.

Sparkling black eyes raised in laughter to the starry skies. Once again, she had followed her heart—but this time she had found herself.

Epilogue

Moonlight spilled through the trees, casting a silver glow on the dark-haired girl and the black wolf. They moved in sync, running through the lush forest.

"It's coming from the portal field." Dreamer's eyes reflected twinkling stars.

Awakened in the night, they had both felt it: strong magic in Ravenswood.

A breeze whispered through the preserve. Adriane could feel Storm watching her, keeping her safe.

Breaking through the thick trees, Adriane came to a stop, Dreamer at her side.

All was still across the field. Mist rose from the forest floor, veiling the trees in a primeval swirl.

Adriane slowly stepped through the tall grass, scanning the trees at the field's edge.

Her stone sparked, and she suddenly reeled, sensing the powerful magic nearby. Dreamer growled low, pointing toward the source.

Hidden in a thick grove of oaks, a shadow moved.

"Who's there?" Adriane called out warily.

Teeth bared, Dreamer crouched, ready to lunge.

Starlight spilled over the lone figure's ragged coat as it stumbled forward, eyes flashing red.

Adriane gasped.

Mrs. Beasley Windor stood hunched, her face twisted into a menacing leer.

Adriane swung into position, jewel flaring with power. "What are you doing here?" the warrior demanded.

Like a puppet, the repulsive figure shuffled toward them. "I believe we have some unfinished business, warrior."

That wasn't Windor's voice. It was the voice of the Dark Sorceress.

"Stay where you are!" Adriane ordered, silver fire coiling around her wrist.

"Your wolf looks quite healthy," Windor sneered, drool hanging from her lip. "As does your jewel."

"Let Windor go," Adriane commanded.

"How else was I supposed to get to you? Your dreamcatcher is stronger than ever."

"What do you want?"

Mrs. Windor lumbered closer to Adriane and Dreamer. "I have something for you."

A brilliant gem lay in her open hands.

Adriane stepped back, the power crystal bathing her tanned face in light. "What kind of trick is this?"

"No trick, warrior." Windor held out the power

crystal. "You have no idea what I risk to bring this crystal to you."

"I'm touched." Adriane could not keep her eyes off the amazing crystal.

"She's insane, you know." The sorceress's voice grated against Windor's throat.

"Takes one to know one."

"We are both served by keeping the power of Avalon out of the witch's hands."

Adriane broke her gaze away. "I don't believe you."

Windor stood in the stark light of the moon.

"You have done what I have only dreamed about," the sorceress said softly. "Taken the magic of the mistwolves. But the path to Avalon is far more dangerous than you can imagine. You think your animals can balance the magic, but each time you use it, there is a price to pay." Windor's eyes glared fire, burning into Adriane's soul. "You cannot have magic without loss. *That* is the only balance."

Adriane listened intently—she had known the dizzying loneliness, the aching and grieving of what it meant to lose what she loved most.

"You asked me what I have lost in my quest for magic," the sorceress hissed. "Everything—even my own sister."

Moonlight cast shimmering beams over the demented figure.

"Why are you telling me this?" Adriane finally asked.

"There may be a way for us to work together to rebuild Avalon."

"You *are* insane!"

It was hard to believe this was coming from the enemy who had nearly destroyed the mistwolves, her friends, and the entire world of Aldenmor.

Yet the crystal was the real thing, she knew it.

"Go ahead, take it." The sorceress's voice oozed like honey.

Dreamer growled as Adriane cautiously stepped forward and grabbed the crystal. "I don't know what you're up to, but whatever it is, my friends and I will be ready."

"We'll see." The sorceress's smile cracked Windor's face into a ghoulish grin.

With a flash, Windor blinked. Horrified, she looked around and took off, screaming into the night.

Adriane took a deep breath, her hands closing around the warm facets of the power crystal.

"Into the great unknown," she murmured, kneeling by Dreamer's side.

Her pack mate nodded, his emerald eyes bright with magic. Dreamer scanned the portal field one last time, then trotted back toward the cottage.

The warrior followed her pack mate into the dark forest, the magic of Avalon lighting her way.

Coming Soon!

Avalon   Quest for Magic # 4

Heart of Avalon
By Rachel Roberts

Avalon needs a healer!

Time is running out—the evil Spider Witch has begun reweaving the magic web, and the fate of Avalon depends on the mages working with their animal friends to recover the missing power crystals.

Yet unless Emily can bond with one special animal, she cannot advance to Level 2 mage like her friends, Kara and Adriane.

When the healer is mysteriously whisked away to a deserted tropical island on Aldenmore, she meets a strange, shapeshifting creature. The creature holds the secret not only to evolving Emily's healing magic, but also to finding the path to Avalon.

But is Emily up to the challenge?

Can the healer find her one true magical animal and fulfill her destiny to heal Avalon?

KIND News Online

Be a kid in Nature's Defense!
Visit KIND News Online at

www.kindnews.org

The website for kids who care about people,
animals and the earth.

Experience even more of the magic:

Become an Avalon Clubhouse member!

To find out more, visit **www.avalonclubhouse.com**

Or write to:
Avalon Clubhouse
P.O. Box 568
Lowell, MA 01853

(Check with your parent or guardian before visiting
any website!)